The
Boy with the
Bronze
Axe

The Boy with the Bronze Axe

KATHLEEN FIDLER

Kelpies
Classics

Illustrations by Edward Mortelmans

Kelpies is an imprint of Floris Books

First published in 1968 by Oliver & Boyd
First published in Kelpies in 2005
This edition published in 2012
Sixth printing 2019
© 1965 Estate of Kathleen A. Goldie

 Also available as an eBook

British Library CIP Data available
ISBN 978-086315-882-7
Printed and bound by MBM Print SCS Ltd. Glasgow

 Floris Books supports sustainable forest management
by printing this book on materials made from wood that
comes from responsible sources and reclaimed material

For my dear friends James and Jean Taggart

Books by Kathleen Fidler

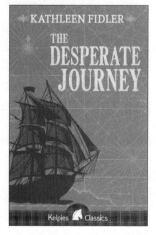

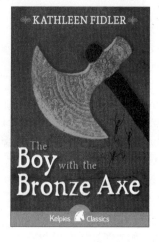

Foreword

In the winter of 1850 a terrible storm struck the coasts of the Orkney Isles. The sea rose higher than it had ever done there within the memory of man. It washed away part of the high sand dunes that fringed the Bay of Skaill and laid bare the ruins of some ancient dwellings, which had been covered by sand. There were seven stone huts connected by passages, which had been paved and roofed. There were signs that there had been more huts, but these had been washed away by the sea. There was also a central paved area which was like a small market place.

People interested in ancient things began to explore and excavate these ruins. It was discovered that there was stone furniture in most of the huts: paved floors, stone hearths, stone beds and cupboards, stone seats, stone water tanks and even stone dressers. When the sand was cleared away treasures of stone hammers, axes, knives, carved stone balls, earthenware bowls and necklaces of bone and animals' teeth were found. The storm had stripped bare a Stone Age village more than three thousand years old.

From the way the Stone Age people had left their treasures in their beds and cupboards and their tools scattered on the floors of their huts, they must have left the settlement in a great hurry. One woman, in her haste to get away, had caught her necklace in a stone doorpost. It broke and the bone "beads" were left lying on the floor.

What caused these Stone Age people to flee from their homes? There were no signs of battle, no corpses slain in a fight, no evidence of fire, save on the hearths. But there was sand, sand everywhere. The dwellings were filled and covered by sand. A great storm must have set the sand dunes moving like the waves of the sea. The villagers fled before the choking, suffocating sandstorm. It took another great storm in 1850 to give back to the world the ancient Stone Age village of Skara Brae.

1. The Boy from the Sea

Kali sat up in her stone bed filled with heather and thrust aside the sheepskin robe which covered her. She listened. From the Bay of Skaill she heard the complaining sharp cries of seagulls. A peewit answered plaintively from the moors to the south, while from the Loch of Skaill there came the honking of swans. Kali knew from all these sounds that the dawn must be reddening in the eastern sky. Her mother still slept in the stone bed-place on the other side of the hearth. Stempsi always slept longer when Birno her husband was away quarrying the stone for the building of the great Ring of Brodgar. Kali's six-year-old brother stirred in the other bed-place. In an instant he was wide awake like a small animal of the wild.

"Kali! Kali! I can hear the swans. Is it time we were going?" he whispered.

Kali hesitated.

"You told me you would take me to the island today if the sun shone," Brockan reminded her.

"We will see first if there is no mist," Kali told him. "Do not wake Mother."

She girdled her sheepskin robe about her with a leather thong. She picked up a bag also made of sheepskin and dropped two flint scrapers into the bottom of it. The fire was still smouldering in the hearth in the centre of the dwelling. Kali carefully placed a couple of peats in the glowing heart of it. That would take care of the fire till her mother woke. The two children tiptoed to the narrow entrance and Kali stooped under the stone doorway to the passage beyond. The entrance to the passage was closed by a slab of stone held in place by a stone bar fixed into holes on each side of the wall. Brockan helped her to lift the bar out and to haul the thin slab aside.

Quietly they crept along the paved passage which curved round their stone house till they reached a gap in the wall, which led upwards and outwards to the daylight. They stood on the sand dune that lay about their house, almost level with the beehive-like roofs of the stone village of Skara. The sun was rising, a half-circle of fire above the horizon. The two children faced about to the west, where the sea moved placidly. The tide was very low and a large stretch of sand was uncovered round the Bay of Skaill.

"Look, Kali! It is just right for us to go." Brockan pointed to the sands in the south, where there rose a group of rocky islets.

Still Kali hesitated. "When Father took me to the rock that is furthest in the sea, he told me I was never to go there alone. It is uncovered only when the tide is very low."

"If we wait for Father to come back from hauling the new stone to the Ring of Brodgar then the tide will not be low any longer. You promised me you would take me to find the large limpets, Kali," Brockan urged her. "You know we can only wade out to that large rock when the tide is very low."

It was two years since Birno had taken Kali to the small island. She still remembered the feast of limpets they had that night and the large crabs that her father had found in the rock crevices. After all, she had been two years younger then. Now she was thirteen years old and well grown. She hesitated no longer.

"Very well! We will go. You must watch your feet over the slippery seaweed," she warned Brockan.

They scampered across the dunes and the wide sandy shore till they came to the chain of rocks stretching out to sea from the south side of the bay. Kali kilted up her sheepskin tunic above the leather girdle. Brockan hitched his tunic up too. Between the islets the sea lapped gently. The tide was very low, a neap tide.

"Now we must wade," Kali said and clutched her sheepskin bag more tightly under her arm. It was drawn together by a plaited cord of strong marram grass threaded through pierced holes.

The children plunged and splashed their way through pools and over the rocks. Once Kali's foot slipped and she almost fell into the channel below.

"I shall have to step carefully when I come back with the heavy bag of limpets," she told Brockan.

At last they reached the island furthest out into the sea. It was little more than a large rock. The limpets clung all round it just below the fringe of green seaweed that marked the level of high tide. Kali handed Brockan a sharp flint with a razor-like edge.

"Come, now! Work quickly! As soon as the tide rises we shall have to go."

"You spoke truth, Kali. The limpets here are much bigger than those on the shore rocks," Brockan said with satisfaction.

The children chipped away with the flint knives. They had to get the edge of the flint knife under the limpet shell and prise it upwards. Their hands grew sore as they worked, but the bag grew heavier.

"We shall have a feast for my father when he comes back from the Ring of Brodgar," Kali said happily.

A few miles from the stone houses of Skara a great stone ring was being built for a temple. Birno had gone to shape the enormous stone the men of Orkney had hewn from the quarries. The tribesmen had only stone and flint axes with which to work. Already men had grown old and died in the labour of hewing and hauling the stones to the Ring of Brodgar. Birno was a clever man at working in stone and he supervised the labour.

"Brockan! There are great crabs in the pools here," Kali told her brother. "Down near the bottom of that gully is the best place to get them."

They climbed down the rocky gully to the pools left by the tide. A big crab scuttled under a shelf of rock.

"Ah! I'll soon have you out of there!" Brockan cried with delight.

He parted the trailers of seaweed. The crab cowered beneath a pebble and waved his great claws menacingly. Kali felt at the bottom of her bag for the small stone axe her father had hewn and polished for Brockan. It was fitted into a handle of antler horn and bound tightly with strips of sheepskin. Every boy of the village carried a stone axe as soon as he was able to use one. She handed it to Brockan; then she snatched the pebble from above the crab. Brockan brought the axe down smartly before the crab could scuttle away. Kali caught hold of the crab by his shell and tossed him into the bag with the limpets. "Mother will boil him in the pot tonight," she laughed gaily.

A small flatfish tried to bury itself under the sand at the bottom of the pool, but Brockan stunned it with a quick blow of the axe. It, too, joined the crab and limpets. The children were so delighted at their catches that they went on searching the pools, clambering up and down among the rocks. They caught two more crabs, and then Kali spotted a small eel in a crack between two rocks. She put a limpet down at the entrance to the crevice. Both children watched, holding their breath. The eel emerged to snatch at the limpet but Kali moved faster still. She pounced and caught him behind the head with her hands. The eel writhed, but Kali held on. She dropped him on a flat rock. Before he could squirm away Brockan's stone hammer dealt him a death blow.

"Here are some great big limpets!" Brockan pointed to a nearby rock. They began chipping away again with their flint knives. They were so absorbed that they lost all track of time. A splash in a near pool made Kali jump round smartly. The water was rising fast in the gully made by the outlet of a small stream from the land. Already the flow of the stream had been driven backwards into a whirlpool by the rising tide. Between them and the shore the waters were lapping and foaming over the rocks.

"The tide has come up!" Kali shouted in horror.

"Oh, Kali! What shall we do?" Brockan looked frightened.

"It's too deep to wade. There's a channel between us and the shore. We'll have to swim for it, Brockan." She looked doubtfully at him. At six years old he was not a very strong swimmer.

"I ... I don't think I can do it, Kali. The waves would batter me against the rocks. You go and leave me here," Brockan stammered.

"No, no! I'll not leave you. I brought you here. I should have remembered what my father told me and not disobeyed. It's my fault. Oh, what shall we do?" Kali cried in desperation.

They looked round about them. Already the sea was churning and foaming between them and the land.

"We'll climb to the top of the rock and shout. Perhaps

someone will hear us at Skara," Kali said, but there was little hope in her heart. The rising wind would drown their shouting, and no one at the little stone village knew where they were.

Even in her fear Kali did not forget to put the flint knives and the stone axe in her sheepskin bag. She hauled it up with her to the top of the spray-drenched rock. Then she and Brockan shouted and shouted till their lungs were fit to burst. No one answered. The blue peat smoke curled lazily from the holes in the beehive-shaped roofs of Skara. The wind carried away their shouts and the roar of the tide drowned their voices. Panic-stricken, they clung to each other as the tide rose higher and higher. A large wave curled slowly over the flat-topped rock and lapped at their feet. Soon it would be impossible to hold on.

The water rose to their ankles. They could hardly keep their balance. Brockan began to sob. Kali held him close to her. How long would it be before the waves overwhelmed them? She turned her face from the land and looked towards the sea. Below them a small creek made a tiny harbour on the seaward side.

"If only my father was at Skara! He would come out with his boat," she wept.

"You could still swim to land, Kali," Brockan told her. "One of us might be saved then."

"No! We will stay here together."

They felt the cold water rise about their legs.

"Shout again! Let's try again!" Kali cried desperately.

Again they faced the land. "Help! Help!" they shouted at the top of their voices, but the wind made mock of their cries.

"Help! Come and save us!" Kali gave one last despairing cry. To her surprise there was an answering hail, but it came to them from over the sea. They sprang round.

There, a few hundred yards away, was a boat, a strange boat to their eyes, but nevertheless a boat. In it a lad was scooping at the water with a broad paddle.

"Try to hold on! I'm coming!" he shouted.

Though Kali could not make out his words properly, the sense of it reached her. She gave a gasp of thankfulness. This must be a god out of the sea, coming to save them.

"Sit down, Brockan. It will be harder for the waves to wash us off if we cling to each other."

The boat came nearer. It was made from a hollowed-out tree trunk. Brockan looked at it in surprise and fear. "I have never seen a boat like that before. It is not like our father's sheepskin boat."

"No, but it is a boat and a strong boat too that will hold all of us." Kali waved her hands and shouted to the lad in the boat. "This way! This way!" She pointed to the entrance to the tiny creek opening up beside them. With a deft turn of his paddle the lad swung his boat towards the rock. The set of the tide brought it nearer, but it seemed as if the boat would be swept past.

"Oh! He cannot reach us!" Brockan cried. "Let's swim to him."

Kali tightened her hold on Brockan. "Wait!" she cried. "You would be pounded to death on the rocks. Look! He is turning to try to reach us."

Once more the boy swung the great dugout canoe. This time the waves and current helped. The boat floated between the protecting pinnacles of rock and into the slightly calmer water of the little creek. A few more strong strokes of the paddle, and he brought his craft alongside the rock.

The boy steadied the craft with his paddle and Kali gave

Brockan a hand into it, then she stepped in carefully herself in order not to disturb the balance of the boat. She still clutched the bag of limpets and crabs.

"Thank you for saving us from the sea, stranger," she said.

The lad pointed towards the sand dunes. "I will put you ashore," he said, using his paddle vigorously. Even without the gesture Kali found she could understand his speech, though it sounded a little different from her own.

"You speak the same words as we do. Are you from this island? I have not seen you before."

The boy shook his head and pointed over the sea. "I come from a long way over the water.

"Did you come alone?" Kali asked in surprise.

"There was a quarrel between our tribe and another one about the right to hunt in a certain place. There was fierce fighting. My father, the chieftain, was killed before my eyes. Most of my tribe were slain."

Kali looked at him in pity.

"They tried to capture me, but I ran faster than they did and hid in a cave on the shore. At sunset they gave up looking for me. In the darkness I managed to reach my father's boat. I launched it and pulled away from the shore. I thought I would land further along the coast, but the wind blew strongly and carried me out to sea.

"How long ago was this?" Kali asked.

The boy held up two fingers. "All night and the next day the wind blew hard and carried me northwards. Sometimes I slept. Sometimes I wakened in the darkness to the howling of the wind and the roaring of the sea. I did not think I would be alive when the second day broke. Then, as the sun rose, the wind lessened and the sea no longer tossed me about. I saw a long low cloud far away that I thought might be land.

I took up my paddle again and steered towards it. As I came near the shore I heard your shouts."

"It was lucky for us that you heard us. Your name, stranger?" Kali asked.

"Tenko."

"I am Kali and this is Brockan, my brother. It is strange that we speak nearly the same tongue."

"There is an old tale in my tribe that some of our people went in their boats to the north and never came back again."

"And there is a tale in our tribe that the people of our island came over the sea from a land in the south," Kali told him in wonder. "There must be some truth in it, when we can understand each other although our words are not all quite the same."

"Where is your home?" Tenko asked.

Kali pointed towards the sand dunes. The wisps of smoke rose from the beehive roofs of the sunken houses. Tenko gave a strong swing of his paddle and urged the boat towards the shore.

Kali looked at Tenko. He was a strong, well-built lad of about fourteen years, bigger than most boys of her tribe. His face was long and narrow and his head round like those of the people of the tribe of Skara. His dark hair grew down to his shoulders, but the ends of it had been lopped off by a flint knife so that it did not straggle. Like Kali and Brockan he was clothed in animal skins, but these were not sheepskins. Tenko's garments were a tunic of some soft supple skin and a cloak from an animal with long dark fur. Kali pointed first to the tunic.

"What animal?" she asked.

"A deer."

"There are deer that roam our hills." She pointed next to the cloak. "But what animal is that?"

"A wolf. I hunted and killed him myself," Tenko told her proudly.

Kali shook her head, puzzled. "I have never seen such an animal on our island. Our men do not hunt often, and then it is only the deer."

"What then do you eat?" Tenko asked, surprised.

"We have herds of sheep and cattle, so we have meat. And we eat limpets and crabs and fish from the sea."

"Do you go hungry in winter?"

Kali shook her head. "Not often. We kill our sheep and salt the meat. Then we keep it in a stone keeping-place under the ground."

They were drawing in to the shore.

"You will come with us to our home?" Kali asked him.

Tenko hesitated. "How will the men of your tribe treat me? Do they not kill strangers?"

"Why should they kill you? You have saved our lives. Besides, how can you be a stranger when you speak as we do?" Kali said.

Still Tenko hesitated. "Perhaps I had better put you on land and go away again."

"But that is foolish," Kali told him. "You cannot go over the sea for ever and ever. What will you eat? Come with us and share our limpets and meat." She shook the bag of shellfish.

Tenko felt the keen pangs of hunger. It was nearly two days since he had eaten the last steak of deer meat he had carried in the pocket of his tunic. The girl was right. Where could he go? He would have to land soon and then he might meet with unfriendly people. This girl, Kali, would speak for him to her tribesmen. Had he not saved them from the sea? The words of an old wise man, a priest of his tribe, came back to him.

"In the great water one will be lost, yet two will be found. Out of this, good will come."

The sea had brought him, the lost one, to Kali and Brockan. It was a sign.

"Very well! I will go with you to your people," he told Kali. He turned the nose of the boat in towards the shore. It grounded and he set foot on the island of Orkney.

2. The Axe of Bronze

The children helped Tenko to haul his boat high up beyond the reach of the tide in the Bay of Skaill. Before Tenko left his boat he reached into the bottom of it and took out his treasures from beneath his wolfskin cloak. There was a light bow of springy birchwood and a bundle of shafts tipped with flint arrowheads. The most precious treasure of all, flat and shining, was a bronze axe fastened by thongs of leather to a haft of wood. Tenko lifted it with reverence. It was almost as dear to him as life itself.

Kali and Brockan looked at it with big eyes.

"That is not like our axes. Our axes are carved out of stone. What is your axe made of?" Kali asked.

"The head is made of bronze."

"Bronze? What is bronze?" Kali asked. "Is it not a kind of stone?"

"No, but it is made out of something that is found in the earth and is melted in a great fire."

Brockan stroked the haft of the axe. "What is this? It is not so hard or cold as stone."

"It is wood."

"Like your boat?" Kali's quick eyes saw the stuff of both was the same. "What is wood?"

"It comes from trees. In my land there are many trees."

"Trees? What are trees?" Brockan asked.

Tenko looked at him with astonished eyes. "Have you no trees growing in your land?"

The children shook their heads, bewildered. Tenko took one of his arrows and with it he drew a tree in the sand, a tree with long branches. Kali and Brockan watched, fascinated. Suddenly Kali clapped her hands. She pointed to the trunk of the tree and to the long hollowed-out boat drawn up on the sand.

"Your boat has come from that?"

"Yes, yes."

"It grows big, big out of the ground?" Kali spread her arms.

"Yes, that is a tree. Surely you have seen a tree?"

Kali shook her head. "We have no big trees like that in our island, but we have tiny ones." She seized the arrow and drew a small gorse bush. Tenko nodded.

"Sometimes, but not often, there are pieces of trees brought ashore by the tide. Once, long ago, a large tree was washed into our bay by a storm. I do not remember it, but Lokar, the old wise man of our tribe, told us about it. His father saw it," Kali told Tenko.

"Did they not make a boat of it?" Tenko asked.

"Yes. That is another of the tales Lokar tells. He said it was not a good boat for it kept rolling over. Three young men set out in it but they never came back again. Lokar said they might have gone to another island."

"There are other islands besides this one, then?" Tenko asked.

"Yes, but we have never been to them. Our boats are not big enough."

"Have you got boats?"

"Yes, but they are only big enough for one man. My father made one of sheepskin stretched over the bones of animals. He uses it sometimes to cross a channel to the rocks so that he can gather limpets," Kali told Tenko.

Brockan was fingering Tenko's axe with interest. He lifted

it and tried the weight of it in his hand. Tenko did not forbid him, but as soon as Brockan laid it down, Tenko picked it up and tucked it away in a big flap-like pocket inside his cloak. Before Brockan could ask another question there came a shout from the village of stone huts just above the sand dunes. Birno had emerged from the narrow opening to the huts and came running towards the children.

"It is my father! He has come back from the Ring of Brodgar," Kali exclaimed.

"Where have you been?" Birno asked. He sounded angry. Then he noticed Tenko. "Who is this?"

"He is a boy from over the sea, Father. He came in a long boat just like the ones Lokar told us about," Kali explained quickly.

Birno looked disbelieving.

"Yes, he did, Father!" Brockan put in. "Look! There is his boat down there." He pointed to the long, dark shape of the boat lying on the beach. Birno cast a quick astonished glance at it.

"Which island are you from, lad? There are no islands here where men build boats like that."

"I am from no island. I come from a great land across the sea to the south. My boat was blown here in a storm."

Birno looked unbelieving and Kali put in quickly, "Lokar told us there was such a land, Father. Do you not remember?" Kali was eager that Birno should accept Tenko with friendship.

"Tenko took us off the rocks just in time before the sea washed us off," Brockan put in, also eager that his father should like their new friend.

"Which rocks?" Birno asked sharply.

Kali hung her head a little. "We ... we went to the far rocks to get limpets for your meal, Father." She pointed to the rocks over which the sea was breaking in clouds of spray. "See, we got crabs and an eel too." She feared her father's anger and, woman-like, she was trying to placate him with the thought of the good meal to come. Birno was not to be beguiled, however.

"You went to the far rocks and took Brockan with you? You disobeyed my word?"

"The tide was very low, Father. I ... I did not think there would be any danger," Kali faltered. "There were so many limpets and crabs that we did not notice the tide rising."

Brockan was too fond of Kali to let her take all the blame. "I asked Kali to take me. And Tenko reached us with his boat and saved us before the waves could wash us off the rock."

A little crowd of people had come out of the stone huts when they heard Birno's voice raised in anger. They stared in astonishment at Tenko.

Birno turned to the boy. "You saved my children from drowning? For that I thank you, stranger. Will you eat with us before you set off back again in your boat to your own land?"

Suddenly Tenko staggered from utter weariness and faintness from hunger. The tossing for two nights and a day in the open boat had left him weak. The cloak he was clutching round him flew open and the axe with the shining head fell to the ground. A murmur of surprise ran round the crowd. A youth a little older than Tenko stooped to pick it up from the ground, but Tenko quickly recovered himself and snatched it up first. He stood there with the axe in his hand, menacing and gleaming. Once again he swayed on his feet, almost fainting. Birno put out an instinctive hand to help him.

"Father, let him sleep in our house tonight. He has not slept and he has not eaten for more than two days," Kali begged Birno.

"Come with me, boy," Birno said. With his arm supporting

Tenko he led the way down the stone passage to his hut. Even in his utter exhaustion, Tenko still clutched his axe. Kali carried the skin cloak he had dropped. Neither of them saw the look of hate and envy that the youth who had tried to pick up the axe gave Tenko. But Brockan caught it out of the corner of his eye.

Stempsi, Birno's wife, gave a cry of surprise when she saw Tenko.

"I will tell you about this boy when we have eaten," Birno said. "Get food now. He has not eaten for two days. Sit there, boy." He indicated the stone bed like a trough that was filled with heather and bracken. Near to the bed was a square hole about a foot deep, lined with slate. It was filled with fresh water. Birno lifted an earthenware bowl from the floor and filled it with water and held it to Tenko's lips. He gulped down the water thirstily.

"More!" he begged, pointing to the bowl. Birno refilled it and Tenko took it into his own hands this time. Colour began to flow back into his cheeks. "That is good," he said.

"Have you been without water for two whole days?" Birno asked.

"No. There is always a horn of water left in the boat in case we cannot easily get back to land. That lasted me till this morning, as I took only a sip at a time. But I have been thirsty since then."

Kali emptied the limpets and shellfish on to a stone slab and began to scrape the limpets out of their shells into a shallow earthenware bowl. She used a tiny flint scraper as a knife. Stempsi took the crabs and eel and wrapped them up in a covering of wet clay which she thrust into the glowing heart of the fire, prodding it into place with the long leg bone of an ox which she used like a poker. There the shellfish would bake while they ate the raw limpets.

The family gathered round the peat fire in the very centre of the house. The smoke escaped through a hole in the thatched roof. Round the fire was a low curb of stone around which were placed larger stones for seats. On these the family sat.

"There is meat too today," Brockan whispered greedily to his sister and pointed to legs of mutton placed on a stone dresser at the side of the hut. "It will be quite a feast." His mouth watered.

Kali offered the dish of limpets to her father first, who signed that she should hand the dish to Tenko.

"Eat well! Do not hold back," he told Tenko.

Tenko took a handful of the limpets and swallowed them hungrily. Birno himself ate some and so did Stempsi.

"Hand the dish to the stranger again," Birno ordered Kali.

Kali did as she was bidden, but Tenko looked doubtfully at the dish. "There is not much left in it," he said, hesitating to put in his hand.

"Kali and Brockan owe you thanks for saving their lives. Today you will eat their share of the food. It will be your reward and their punishment for going to the rocks when I had forbidden it," Birno said sternly.

Kali hung her head. Brockan began to sniffle. The tears came into Kali's eyes, nevertheless she held up her bowl to Tenko. "Please, eat," she said in a low voice.

"I ... I cannot." Tenko's voice faltered. "Let Kali and Brockan eat too," he begged Birno.

Birno's face softened. "Not of the limpets or crabs. I have spoken my word about that. They may eat of the meat, though, because you ask it."

Kali looked gratefully at Tenko. Brockan cheered up at once, though he still looked regretfully at the limpets.

While the crabs and eel were baking in their clay wrapper

in the fire, Stempsi handed the mutton bones to everyone. Earlier she had thrust the meat among the hot stones in the fire, and though the outside was scorched, the inside meat was almost raw. That did not worry anyone. The family was used to eating its meat either raw or partly burned. They all gnawed at the bones with relish, their strong white teeth tearing the meat away.

Tenko smiled happily for the first time as he sat on a stone beside the fire. He had been asked by this family to sit at their hearth and eat their meat. Among his people this meant that they accepted a stranger as a friend. No doubt it would be the same in Birno's tribe.

When they had done eating they relaxed and Birno seemed inclined to ask questions of Tenko. "You carry a strange axe, Tenko. Will you let me see it?"

Tenko handed it to him. Birno examined it curiously.

"What kind of stone is used for the head?" he asked.

"It is not stone nor flint," Tenko told him. "It is made out of two substances found among the rocks in a land that lies far to the south. They are tin and copper and they show like streaks in the rocks. The tin and copper are melted together in a hot fire and poured into a shape like an axe head hollowed in the sand. That is what my father told me."

"Did your father not make it for you?"

"No. We have no tin or copper in our land, but my father's father came from a tribe in the south. He had two axes with him, that he had got by trading skins with men from across the sea that lies far away to the south. My father had one axe. He gave the other to me."

Birno felt the edge with his thumb. "It is far sharper than our stone axes. Take care of it, Tenko."

"While I live I will not be parted from it," Tenko said.

Stempsi drew the clay wrappers from the fire by the long piece of bone and left them to cool. While they were waiting, Tenko looked about him. Bone rafters made the roof, and turfs had been laid upon them to thatch them, but a large hole had been left above the hearth for a chimney. Through this the smoke swirled. At one side of the hut was a stone dresser built of flat slabs resting on pillars of stone.

"You have beds and a dresser just as we have, but ours are made of wood from the trees that grow round about our houses," he remarked to Birno.

"Wood like your boat?" Kali put in.

"Yes. We make nearly all our things of wood."

"We have no trees on this island. That is why we make things of stone and bone. They will last many many lives and our people will use them long after us," Birno said. "Our wise man, Lokar, has told us about trees, though. To him all the stories of our tribe have been handed down. He is our storyteller during the long winter evenings round the fire."

Birno broke away the clay covering from the crab. He broke the shell with a stone and pulled away the two large claws. These he gave to Tenko. He was about to hand Stempsi her share when there came the sound of feet along the narrow entrance to the hut. Korwen, the youth who had given Tenko the look of dislike, poked his head through the door.

"Birno! I am sent to ask you to come to the meeting place. The men of Skara have gathered together."

Birno frowned. At first he stayed where he was; then he dropped the crab into a bowl and rose to his feet.

"Very well! I will come."

Stempsi lifted the bowl of shellfish on to the stone dresser and covered it with a piece of slate so that no rats could get at it while the family slept.

"Into your bed, Brockan," Stempsi said. "Tonight Tenko will share the bed with you and Kali will sleep in the little bed at the foot of mine."

Tenko's eyes were already closing and his head nodding. He had been so long without much sleep and he was exhausted by his battle with the sea. He willingly stretched himself on the springy bed of heather and bracken. Brockan climbed in beside him and Stempsi stretched soft sheepskins over them. Tenko was still clutching the two large crab claws in his left hand. Before he slept he gave them to Brockan.

"Wait till all is quiet and then give one of them to Kali."

"But Father –" Brockan began.

"Ssh! The crab claws are mine now. Your father gave them to me, so I can do as I wish with them. Eat one yourself and there is one for Kali."

Soon Tenko was fast asleep, but his right hand still clutched his bronze axe, which lay among the heather between him and Brockan.

Stempsi swept the hearth with a brush of bracken and laid fresh peats on the fire so it would smoulder away till morning. The new peats threw a black shadow over the hut and its occupants. Stempsi too went to her bed. There was no knowing when Birno might return. Sometimes the men talked long into the night. Soon she too fell into a doze.

Brockan stayed awake, sucking and nibbling at the crab claw, rolling the meat over in his mouth. Across on the other side of the fire-hearth Kali stirred restlessly in the smaller bed.

"Sss! Kali!" Brockan hissed.

"What is it?" Kali whispered back

"Catch! It is from Tenko."

The second crab claw whirled through the air above the fire and into Kali's bed. She felt around till she found it. When she discovered what it was she gave a little exclamation of delight. Soon she too was busy pushing her tongue into the crevices of the claw. She looked gratefully in Tenko's direction, but he was drenched in sleep. Soon Kali's eyes closed too, but not before she had hidden the claw among the heather of the bed. It was now a treasured possession. Only Brockan stayed awake beside Tenko, his bright eyes gleaming when an occasional flicker of firelight caught them.

In the centre of a group of stone huts was a paved space open to the sky. To it four passages led from all the stone huts that made the village of Skara. This was the meeting place, where the men of the village gathered to decide matters which affected them all. When Birno got there he found the other men awaiting him. In the place of honour was Lokar with his long white beard, the wise old man of the tribe. Lokar sat on a large stone slab but the other men sat cross-legged on the ground. Lokar looked up when Birno joined them, but said nothing. The evening light was fading but they could still see each other as the meeting place was open to the sky. Birno took his place in the circle.

"Why have you all met here?" he asked. "I did not call you." It was Birno's right as head of the tribe to call the men to a meeting.

"No, Birno, you did not call us," a man called Tresko replied, "but I spoke to Lokar and he agreed that it was wise that we should meet and talk together."

Lokar inclined his head.

"What have we to talk about that calls for all the men of the village to sit here?" Birno asked in a haughty voice.

Tresko spoke up. "It is about the stranger who came here today from out of the sea. Surely that is a matter for us all?"

"Why should it be? I have taken him into my house," Birno was beginning hotly when Lokar interrupted him in a quiet voice.

"You have taken him into your house, Birno, and it is a law of our tribe that you must answer for him."

"Lokar speaks the truth. You have had time to talk with the lad. What do you know of him? Is he a spirit from the sea or is he a man like ourselves?" Tresko asked.

Birno looked at him contemptuously. "What do you fear? He is just a boy like your son Korwen, though not so old."

"Where did he come from?" Tresko demanded.

"He came over the sea from a great land far to the south. Lokar knows there is such a land."

Lokar nodded. "Yes, all the old tales of our tribe tell us there is a land beyond the noonday sun. Long ago our people came from it in boats made from trees, like that boat the lad came in today."

There was silence for a minute, then Tresko spoke again. "This boy might have been sent to spy out our land. When he has learned all about us he will go back and bring mighty warriors to fight us."

Birno threw back his head and laughed. "It is you who should be telling us tales, Tresko, not Lokar. The lad is harmless. He was blown over the sea by a storm."

"Why then should he come armed, carrying an axe with a shining head such as we have never seen before?" Tresko asked. "For all we know there might be magic in the axe. He could bewitch us all with it."

"You speak stupidly," Birno said briskly. "I asked Tenko about it. He told me there is a way of making such axes out of strange material found among the rocks, but he has never seen it done. His father got two axes from a man in a tribe far to the south."

"Has he given you the axe?" Tresko asked.

"No, I have not asked him for it."

Tresko gave a sneering laugh.

"Listen, Tresko!" Birno said hotly. "That boy saved the lives of my children. Why should I reward him by taking the axe from him? We all give axes to our sons as soon as they are old enough to handle them. Tenko had his from his father, who perished in a battle."

No one noticed Korwen slip away from the outer circle of youths gathered in the shadow, listening.

Birno and Tresko glowered at each other.

"It would be better if Birno took the axe and got rid of the lad. He could turn him adrift in his boat," Tresko said.

"His boat! You are foolish, Tresko. That boat is bigger and stronger than any of ours. If he becomes one of our tribe his boat will be useful to us."

"Then let us take the boat," Tresko said.

A murmur of argument ran round the circle of men, but Lokar held up his hand.

"Birno cannot reward good by evil. That is against our law. But he can ask Tenko for the use of his boat if the lad becomes one of our tribe."

"That I will do," Birno agreed.

"And the axe? What about the axe?" Tresko asked. "It is a better weapon than any of ours. It would not do for the youth to use it against us."

"Birno must give his word that he will take the axe from Tenko if he threatens any of us with it," Lokar decided.

"If Tenko lifts the axe against any of us it shall be taken from him, even if I have to use it against him myself,"

Birno promised. "I will speak for him as for one of my own family."

While the dispute was going on Korwen crept along the main passage, the roofed street of the little stone village, and into the narrow passage that led to Birno's house. At night the openings to these passages were closed by slabs of stone held in place by stone bars which rested in sockets in the inner walls. Tonight, though, the slabs were not in place as the men were all at the meeting place.

Korwen reached the narrow paved passage into Birno's house. Here he paused and listened. He could hear the deep breathing of the sleepers. Cat-like, he crouched on all fours and crept along the low passage. He entered the hut near the small bed where Kali was asleep. She did not stir.

There was a faint glow from the peat fire on the hearth. It was enough to enable Korwen to see – and be seen! Brockan was still wide awake and sucking at his crab claw. He watched Korwen tiptoe past the hearth. What did he want? Why had he come creeping in like that? Brockan half closed his eyes and feigned sleep.

Korwen stood still by Brockan's and Tenko's bed for a long time. Then he slipped a hand into the bed and began to feel among the heather. In a flash Brockan knew what he was after. The axe! It lay between him and Tenko. He pretended to stir as if in sleep and Korwen drew back a few steps. Brockan turned to face outwards but he felt with his hand behind him till he gripped the wooden haft of the axe. Then Brockan waited, eyes closed, breathing as if he were asleep.

Korwen drew nearer again and began to feel with his hands along the foot of the bed. The axe was not there. He tried the head of the bed next, keeping his hands away from Tenko's face. Not there either! Then it must lie on one side or the other of the sleeping Tenko. Korwen leaned over the boys.

Brockan could bear it no longer! With a shriek he sat up with the axe in his hand and brought it down on Korwen's arm. The blood spurted. Korwen gave a yell and jumped back.

Tenko was instantly awake, like an animal at the approach of danger. He leaped out of bed. Korwen made for the passage but Tenko was too quick and grabbed him. Kali was suddenly wide awake too. She rushed over to the fire and impaled a glowing peat on the end of a long bone used for a poker. The peat burst into flame as she thrust it almost into Korwen's face. Korwen drew hurriedly back.

"So it's you, Korwen?" Kali exclaimed.

Stempsi was out of her bed too. "What are you doing here, Korwen, creeping in like a thief?"

"He was stealing Tenko's axe," Brockan shouted.

In a quick writhing movement Korwen slipped from Tenko's grasp. Terrified, he bumped his way along the narrow passage. Tenko seized the axe from Brockan and ran after him. Korwen had the advantage of Tenko because he knew the way. With Tenko at his heels he emerged into the wider passage and fled along to the meeting place. There he burst into the astonished circle of men with Tenko hot behind him, flourishing his bronze axe. After both of them Kali and Brockan came running.

The men leaped to their feet. Korwen dashed to Tresko and hid behind him, blood dripping from the gash in his arm. There was shouting and confusion. Birno seized Tenko's upraised arm and swung him about. "What is all this?" he demanded.

"He tried to steal my axe," Tenko accused Korwen.

"He has struck my son with the axe! Look at the cut on his

arm," Tresko cried. "Now you must keep your word, Birno, and take the axe from him and cast the stranger into the sea."

"I did not strike him! No one shall take my axe from me!" Tenko declared fiercely, clutching his axe more tightly.

"How did Korwen come by the cut in his arm then?" Tresko shouted.

"I struck him!" Brockan pushed his way through the circle of men to the centre of the ring. "I hit Korwen with Tenko's axe."

"I do not believe it!" Tresko cried.

"It is true!" Kali said. "I saw Brockan with the axe in his hand. He caught Korwen when he tried to steal it."

Tresko was furious. "No woman-child has the right to speak at our meetings. Turn her away!"

"Be silent, every one of you!" Lokar had mounted on his stone and stood with upraised hand, a tall commanding figure. "Let the children speak. You first, Brockan."

"I was awake and I saw Korwen creep into our hut like a shadow. I pretended to be asleep. When he felt about in the heather of our bed I knew he was searching for Tenko's axe. I had my hand on the axe and I brought it down on his arm."

"And you, Kali?"

"I snatched a peat from the fire and by its light I saw Tenko grappling with Korwen and Brockan shaking the axe."

"The stranger struck me! Tenko struck me!" Korwen yelled.

Kali turned on him. "That is a lie! You are a liar as well as a thief, Korwen! If Tenko had struck you with the axe, he would have severed your arm from your body."

"We will prove Kali's words," Lokar intervened. "Here is the leg of a sheep I meant to cook for my meal. Put it on this stone slab. Now, take the axe, Brockan, and strike with it. You are to use all your strength."

Brockan lifted the axe and brought it down with all the power of his six-year-old arms. A deep gash appeared in the leg, but that was all.

"Now you, Tenko!"

Tenko lifted the axe above his head, poised it and swung it with all his strength. It cut through the flesh and into the bone with a sharp crack, and the bone lay severed in two. A gasp went up from the circle of men.

"You have your answer, Tresko and Korwen," Lokar told them. "Kali and Brockan have spoken the truth."

"My son has been wounded. There is a law in our tribe that blood shall be answered by blood," Tresko cried wildly. "Brockan shall answer for this. Korwen shall strike at him with the axe."

There was a sudden silence among the men. They knew this was the law of their tribe. Birno looked at Brockan, so very pale and so very small, standing with clenched fists and mouth tightly pursed.

"Our law also says that one of a family can take the punishment for another. I will take the punishment for my son. He is too small," Birno declared.

Tenko sprang into the centre of the ring. "What Brockan did to Korwen was for me. Therefore I will answer with my blood in Brockan's place." He thrust the axe into Korwen's hand. "Go on! Strike me!"

"Wait!" Lokar strode into the ring. "You are to strike Tenko no harder than Brockan struck you. If you wound him more deeply, then you must answer for it, Korwen."

"I ... I will not ..." Korwen began, backing away.

"Your father has claimed your right by the law of our tribe. You must strike a blow," Lokar insisted.

"Go on! Strike!" Tenko challenged him.

Korwen aimed a feeble, half-hearted blow at Tenko, who stood still as a stone to receive it. The axe glanced off his arm, leaving only a scratch which bled a little.

"That is enough. The law has been kept," Lokar decreed.

Korwen threw the axe into the centre of the ring. Tenko picked it up. His voice rang out challengingly, "By Korwen's blow I have become a brother to Brockan. I take Birno as my father and his family as my family." Tenko looked straight at Tresko. "Whoever attacks them attacks me. For I will fight if the need arises."

Tresko mumbled in his beard some words that no one could hear. Korwen hung his head and was silent.

Lokar spoke again. "The law has been fulfilled. Tenko is now one of the tribe of Skara. Let there be peace now and go you all to your huts."

3. The Day of the Eagle

The following day Birno's family woke with the coming of light as it filtered through the wide hole in the roof which let the smoke out. Stempsi rose first, poking the peats into a blaze with the leg bone of an ox. She raked out the embers to a smouldering glow and set a large earthenware bowl among them. In the bowl was a stew of pieces of mutton. Kali rose when she heard her mother stirring and fetched another large bowl from the stone dresser.

"Where are you going?" Tenko asked as she passed his bed.

"To milk our cows."

"Wait for me! I will come with you."

Tenko pulled his wolfskin cloak about him.

"Can you milk a cow?" Kali asked him.

Tenko grinned at her. "In my tribe over the sea the men go hunting, not milking cows."

"Now you are one of our family you can make yourself useful," Kali retorted. "There is another bowl on the stone dresser. Bring it with you."

The early mists of morning swirled round the two figures as they climbed the sand dunes to the two small fields behind the settlement. The cows and sheep were kept there during the night in enclosures bounded by a stone wall. Already Salik the herdsman was there. He grunted a sleepy greeting to Kali, and then woke up at the sight of Tenko.

"Ah! Your new brother, the stranger from over the sea!" he said.

Tenko nodded warily. He wondered how the men of the tribe would regard him after the previous night.

"You did well at the meeting place last night," Salik commented. "Now let us see if you can do as well with the milking. I should let him try his hand on the black cow, Kali." There was a twinkle in Salik's eye.

"I will do that." There was a twinkle in Kali's eye too. She led Tenko to the black cow. "There! Kneel beneath her and milk her into that bowl."

Kali busied herself with another cow and under the pressure of her accustomed fingers the milk began to flow readily into her bowl. But Tenko was having difficulty with the black cow. As soon as he had placed the bowl beneath her and knelt down, she moved away. Tenko was left kneeling and looking up at the open sky.

Salik chuckled. "No, no! The milk does not come like rain from heaven. It comes from the cow."

Tenko was annoyed at first; then he joined in the laugh against himself. He tried once again. This time the black cow stood still but there was a wicked look in the corner of her eye. She began to yield her milk, but when the bowl was half full she suddenly became restive. She kicked up her hind legs and sent a shower of dirt into the bowl. Then she moved away again, overturning the bowl with her foot.

Tenko was furious and caught hold of the cow by the tail. Kali moved her bowl and left her own cow.

"Easy now, Tenko! If you make the cow angry she will give no more milk."

She rescued the upturned bowl, wiped it out with a

handful of clean grass and resolutely set to work on the black cow herself.

"It looks so easy when you milk her," Tenko said ruefully. "I hate to be defeated by anything."

"Come, then, and kneel beside me and when I release my hold you go on milking her," Kali suggested.

Tenko did as he was told and took over the milking from Kali. The cow remained docile and at last the bowl was half-filled.

"That is as much as she will give," Kali told Tenko.

Tenko came from beneath the cow with the bowl. He looked ruefully from Kali's bowl to his own. "I am not very good at the milking," he said.

"No doubt you are better at the hunting," she laughed.

They returned to the little stone village. Stempsi was kneeling at the peat fire. She was grilling streaks of mutton at the end of her long pointed bone poker. As she cooked each one she set it on a slate slab to cool a little. Birno was already tearing at his meat with strong white teeth. Brockan was gnawing the meat from a bone.

Stempsi looked up when the two children came in. They set the two dishes of milk down on the dresser. Stempsi eyed Tenko's half-filled bowl. "There is not so much milk as usual," she said.

Tenko coloured. "That is my fault. I am not used to milking cows."

Birno guffawed in amusement. "So the black cow got the better of you?"

Tenko looked vexed, but Kali spoke for him. "In his own country the men do not herd cattle and milk cows. They are hunters."

Birno looked at Tenko with interest. "There may be hunting for you to do here. Some animal or bird has been attacking the lambs on the hillsides when we pasture them there. Kill the attacker for us and we shall believe you are a hunter."

"I will go out with the herdsmen and do what I can," Tenko said quietly. "I have my arrows, but I have no bow. That was washed out of my boat in the sea storm. There are no trees here from which I can cut another bow?"

"There are bushes by the Lake of Skaill. Their shoots will bend but do not break easily," Birno told him.

"You have seen bows and arrow, then?"

"Yes, I have seen them. Some of the tribes on the hills in the centre of our island hunt the deer. We trade cowhides with them for their deer horns. See!" Birno lifted a stone axe from the keeping-place hollowed out of the wall beyond his bed. His stone axe was wedged into a piece of deer antler used as a haft. Lines were chiselled on the stone in a pleasing pattern of squares and diagonals over the centre of the axe-head.

Tenko turned it over in his hand. "It is beautifully carved," he said with admiration.

"My father is the best stone carver in the island," Brockan told him proudly.

"You will need a bowstring too," Birno said, returning to the matter of Tenko's bow. "That is easily found." He felt again in the keeping-place. "Here are some sheep's sinews. They will stretch to a bow, see? Kali and Brockan will take you to the lake. You can cut your bush shoots there."

"Then I will make my new bow today," Tenko said gladly.

"It is on the way to the hill of Gyran, where we are to pasture the sheep. It is our turn to look after the Skara flock today," Kali said.

"You, as my new son, will go with them," Birno decided.

"I will do that," Tenko said, well pleased to be called Birno's son.

They finished their breakfasts of mutton and milk.

"As you go to the herds you will pass through the village, Tenko. Speak with all the people you see," Birno instructed him.

Tenko frowned a little. "Must I do that? They may not wish to speak with me, because I am a stranger."

"You are no longer a stranger apart. You are one of our tribe now and you will act as one of the tribe," Birno said firmly. "You will speak in peace to my people."

Tenko nodded his head obediently.

The three children made their way along the passage to the meeting place. There Lokar, the old wise man, was sitting in the sun. Tenko did not hesitate. He went up to him but respectfully waited till Lokar spoke first to him.

"Well, Tenko, son of Birno?" Lokar said with a smile.

"I thank you, Lokar, for speaking for me before the tribe last night."

"As long as you obey the laws of our tribe and do your duty as a son of Birno, you will have my good word, Tenko." He laid his hand on Tenko's shoulder and stooped and looked him in the eyes. "Go in friendship among my people and yours, Tenko."

Already the people of the settlement were going about their work for the day. Some women were sitting on the sand dunes just outside the huts. With flint scrapers they were busy scraping clean the inside of sheepskins and cowhides. Others, with bone needles, were piercing holes and fastening skins together by threads made from animal tendons. These would be tunics and cloaks for their families.

A midden heap was built up round the outer walls of the settlement. It contained limpet shells, animal bones, scraps of food mingled with ashes from the peat fires. An unpleasant odour rose from it, which might have been worse but for the peat ash, but the people of Skara did not appear to notice it. Perhaps they had lived beside it for too long. The midden served to strengthen the stone walls of the huts against the strong west wind.

In a hut near the wall Lemba the potter had his workshop. He was busy shaping the wet clay into dishes and bowls. With his thumb he made a narrow lip round each bowl, marking it with the claw of a bird. Then he drew a pattern of lines. Where other huts had a stone dresser Lemba's had a stone oven. Below it was a fire of glowing red peats. Clay dishes had been set to dry beside it. They watched Lemba stack them into the oven to bake them into earthenware. He looked round when at last he became aware of the children.

"Hullo, Tenko!" he said with a friendly grin. "Are you coming to learn how to make bowls?"

Tenko smiled back but shook his head. "No, I am going with Kali and Brockan to herd the flocks. You are a good potter, though. I like this bowl very much." Tenko picked up one with a pattern of spiral lines upon it. "I have never seen a pattern like this before."

"No. That is a pattern out of my own head. I do not always keep to the old patterns of my tribe. I like to try new things," Lemba told him.

"I wish I had a bowl like that," Tenko said as he handed it back.

"Some day, maybe, I will make you one like it, when you have done a deed which deserves it," Lemba said lightly. He looked hard at Tenko. "But you are carrying arrows under your arm? That does not look much like a herdsman."

For a moment Tenko looked sad. "In my land over the sea my father was a great hunter and he was teaching me all the things he knew. Now he is no more and Birno has become my father, so I must learn new ways." Then, like the boy he was, he grew cheerful again. "All the same, there may be a chance to do some hunting of the creature that is attacking the flocks, once I have made a new bow."

"Good hunting then, Tenko!" Lemba laughed. He continued drawing patterns on the newly-made bowls.

Other men were ready to set out with Birno over the grasslands to the east.

"They are going to work with my father at hewing a new stone for the temple to the Sun God which they are building at Brodgar," Kali explained.

Before they left, the stoneworkers greeted Tenko. "Good day, son of Birno." Tenko spoke respectfully to them all in turn. Only Tresko and Korwen held aloof, scowling. Tenko took no notice of them.

The children left the village and went to the stone-walled sheep paddocks. The animals were bleating inside, anxious to go out to the new pastures.

"Help me to lift the stone away, Tenko," Kali asked.

Together they shifted the large stone slab that did duty for a gate. The sheep came pouring through the gap. Lifting their arms and shouting, the children urged the flock along and over the low hill towards the Loch of Skaill. Now and again they stopped to let the sheep rest and nibble at the grass. They topped a rise and came on the shining, placid Loch of Skaill. On the shore and leaning over the lake was a clump of osiers.

"There are the long shoots for your bow," Kali pointed out. She took a flint knife from the bag she carried with her and handed it to Tenko. Tenko ran down to the willow bushes and carefully selected two of the shoots which looked supple. He cut them out near the base and then bent them across his knee to test their springiness.

"Yes, these will do," he told Kali.

Kali was carrying the lengths of animal sinews in her bag. She selected one that was smooth and even. Tenko nodded approval. With his flint knife he notched one of the osier wands at each end. Then he inserted the end of the tendon into it and knotted it so it would not slip out again. He did the same with the other end. Now he had a stringed bow. He pulled it gently apart and inserted an arrow. Yes, it was springy enough. He took aim at a clump of heather. In a second his arrow was quivering, point buried in the centre of the clump.

"It is not so strong as the bow I had, but it shoots truly and it will serve," Tenko said.

They turned southwards, driving the flock before them. The land rose in green slopes curling round between two low hills.

"That is Gyran," Kali said, pointing out the easterly hill. "We will pasture the sheep on the slopes this side. There are plenty of young heather shoots for them to eat, besides the grass. We will let the sheep go free now."

The sheep began to scatter over the hill slope. The children sat down on a little outcrop of rocks to watch them. Below them the land sloped to the Loch of Skaill. When they looked westward they could see the beehive roofs of Skara and the peat smoke curling up from them. Behind Skara lay the wide curve of the Bay of Skaill. The white sand of its southern shore gleamed in the sun and the grey slaty rocks of its northern point stood out against the blue-grey sky. Headland after headland stretched away till lost in the mist, the deep blue sea curling and creaming at their rocky feet. The sun mounting high in the heavens warmed the grass. From the clumps of flowering gorse came the hum of bees.

Kali and Brockan stretched themselves on the grass, but not Tenko.

"I am going to practise shooting with my new bow. Then I shall be ready," he said darkly.

"Ready for what?" Brockan asked him.

"For the enemy that takes the lambs." Tenko had not forgotten Birno's words.

He selected a soft clump of gorse about two hundred paces away. He fitted an arrow to his bow and looked carefully along the shaft. Then he let fly. The bow twanged. The arrow struck very near the centre of the gorse bush.

"That was a fine shot, Tenko!" Brockan exclaimed, sitting up to watch.

"It will need to be better still," Tenko replied critically.

"You stay there! I'll fetch your arrows back," Brockan offered.

For close on an hour Tenko practised with his new bow and Brockan ran backwards and forwards with his shot arrows.

"Would you like a shot?" Tenko asked Brockan at last.

Brockan's eyes sparkled. "Could I? Could I?" he asked eagerly.

"Stand erect, a little sideways like this. Hold the bow at the full stretch of your left arm. Fit the arrow with the point to the middle of the bow and the notch at the end of it into the cord. Now draw back the cord as far as you can till the bow bends. Keep your elbow up! Good! Now let the bow go with a snap."

Brockan did as he was told. The arrow fell a little short of the bush but in a direct line.

"That is good, very good! Now, try for yourself. I will fetch the arrows back."

Brockan glowed with delight. He listened to all Tenko said and tried hard to shoot straight. A word of praise now and again from Tenko flushed his face with joy. His admiration for Tenko was growing fast into a brotherly affection. Kali watched them both with a gentle smile on her lips. She kept casting a wary eye upon the straggling sheep. They were nibbling away contentedly, the lambs following their mothers and digging under them for their warm milk.

At last Tenko retrieved the final arrow and he and Brockan flung themselves down on the ground beside Kali. She cast a glance at the sun. It was high overhead.

"It is time to eat," she decided. From the skin bag she drew out pieces of cold meat and a handful of mussels gathered from the shore that morning.

They were finished eating when there was a whirr of wings over the hill behind them. A sudden wind fanned their faces.

"What is that?" Brockan cried in alarm.

A huge dark bird was planing down over the flock. Its neck was outstretched and its great claws were ready to grab.

"It's an eagle!" Kali cried, terrified.

Tenko sprang to his feet and in one swift movement he fitted an arrow to his bow. Then the eagle pounced!

There was one ewe with newly-born twin lambs. She did her best to defend them, stamping at the eagle and lowering her horns at him but she could not keep the eagle from both lambs at once. He was swifter and dug his claws into the neck of a tiny lamb before she could wheel to defend it. The poor little creature gave a horrible screech. The eagle began to rise in the air. Tenko shot his arrow, but by then the eagle was rising so swiftly that his aim missed.

"Oh, why did you not shoot more quickly?" Kali cried.

"Because the ewe was between me and the eagle," Tenko said. "I might have killed the ewe. I had to wait till the bird rose."

"Oh, the poor little lamb!" Kali wept. "It will be torn to pieces by that great bird. What will my father say when he hears we have lost a lamb? And that terrible bird will not be satisfied with one lamb!"

"What did you say?" Tenko grabbed her by the wrist.

"The eagle will come back for another lamb. When he takes one so easily it makes him bold."

"Then we will wait for him," Tenko said grimly. "We will hope the eagle does come back today."

"We may have to wait a long time. He will have to eat that lamb first," Kali said unhappily.

"He may have a family to feed. It is the time of year when young birds are hatched. In that case he may need more meat," Tenko told them. "In the craggy mountains of my land there are many eagles. They build their nests among the rocks."

"There is another island with great hills which lies to the south. The eagle could have come from there. If he did, it will take him a long time to come back again." Kali shook her head as if she doubted that the eagle would ever return.

"He has strong wings and an eagle is swift in flight. He made an easy kill here. He will remember that. Birds have long memories for places where they get their food," Tenko said wisely. "It is not the first time he has taken lambs from your flock. We will still wait and watch. We will bring the sheep closer in beside us."

They went round the flock herding them in closer to the rocks where they had been sitting. Kali went down to the bank where a little stream burst forth and brought back water for them all in earthenware cups. Then they settled down to wait.

The sun was westering. The little flock seemed uneasy. It was as though they knew one kill had been made and they waited for another. The ewe which had lost her lamb bleated constantly and would not let the other twin lamb out of her sight. There was anguish in her bleating. The clouds began to blow in from the sea and to cast dark shadows on the hill of Gyran. Kali shivered when the warm sun disappeared behind them. Tenko watched the sky to the southward. It was to the south the eagle had flown. Brockan watched too, but he looked more to the east. It was Brockan who first saw the hovering speck in the sky.

"Look, Tenko!" he said in a whisper, almost as if the great bird could hear him.

The speck grew larger, nearer. Tenko stood up quietly and fitted an arrow to his bow. He shielded his eyes to watch. Nothing must impair his aim this time.

"Keep very still, Brockan! Take care not to cry out, Kali!" Tenko cautioned her. "I want the eagle to come in close and settle on its lamb. When its eyes are fixed on the lamb, then I will shoot."

The speck had grown into a huge winged bird. The beat of its wings echoed down the hill. The flock sensed the approach of its enemy and faced uneasily this way and that. Ewes tried to gather their lambs under their bodies and the lambs sucked frantically at their mothers, trying to draw comfort and security from the warm taste of their milk.

The flapping of the wings ceased. The eagle hovered a hundred feet above the flock, eyes looking this way and that. The little group by the rocks remained as if carved from stone.

Slowly the eagle planed down till he was just a few feet above the frightened flock which kept turning about, clustering close for greater safety. Suddenly the fierce eyes spied a single lamb on the outskirts of the flock nearest to the watchers. With outstretched claws the eagle dropped like a stone on the lamb. In that instant Tenko's bow twanged.

The eagle's claws were already searching the wool of the

lamb to get a firm hold. For a second the bird raised his head and looked towards the children. In that moment the arrow transfixed the eagle's throat. He fell, a mass of beating, quivering wings, among the sheep.

Tenko dropped his bow and snatched the bronze axe from the deep pocket of his deerskin tunic. Another second, and he was striding among the flock. The eagle was lying in a circle of grass. The sheep had scattered from him on all sides and then turned to watch their fallen enemy. Blood welled from the place in his neck where the arrow still quivered. As Tenko approached the eagle gave a feeble flutter, trying to raise himself on his wings and to strike at his enemy. Tenko rushed upon him with the axe and struck one blow.

Under the eagle's claws the lamb still squealed. Tenko cautiously prodded the eagle with the axe to make sure he was really dead. The great bird did not stir. Then Tenko looked at the lamb. The claws were tangled in the curly wool but, save for a scratch, the lamb was unhurt. Gently Tenko pulled the wool clear of the extended claws. The lamb bleated piteously, fearing yet another enemy. A ewe bleated in answer. Tenko examined the little creature and then set it down gently on its spindly legs. It made one frantic rush at the ewe and thrust its head beneath her for comforting milk. She turned and nuzzled it.

Kali and Brockan came running up.

"He's dead! The eagle's dead!" Brockan cried, jumping up and down. "That was a wonderful shot, Tenko!"

"You've saved the lamb! He's still alive. Tenko, you are indeed a hunter," Kali told him with great respect.

Tenko was pleased, but he tried not to show it. "We must take the eagle back with us to show your father at Skara," he said.

"It is a great weight of a bird. It will be heavy to carry," Kali told him doubtfully.

"Nevertheless I am going to carry him," Tenko declared. "You take my bow and arrows, Brockan, and you carry my axe and cloak, Kali."

He pulled the arrow from the eagle's throat. He took the still-warm bird by the legs and heaved it on to his back. The eagle's head flopped helplessly.

"Round up the sheep. We will go now," Tenko said in a voice of triumph.

When they reached the fields above Skara they penned the sheep. Tenko, with aching shoulders, dead weary but still triumphant, staggered into the meeting place. Kali and Brockan followed, bearing his weapons with the pride of those returning from a war. The men were home from their work at the stone quarry. They jumped to their feet at the sight of Tenko.

"What have you there, Tenko?" Birno cried.

Tenko flung the eagle from his aching shoulders. "Here is the killer of your lambs! He will kill no more."

"An eagle. The lad has killed an eagle!" The cry went up all round the meeting place. Women and children came running from the houses.

"You have done well, my son!" Birno declared with pride.

"It was a good wind that blew you to our shore, Tenko," Lokar told him.

The men pressed round Tenko, patting him on his shoulders. Only Tresko and Korwen held aloof.

Lemba the potter left the circle round Tenko. He dashed to his workshop and came running back with a bowl in his hand. It was the one with the spiral markings that Tenko had admired that morning.

"Take it, Tenko," he said, thrusting the bowl into Tenko's hand. "You have today done a deed which deserves it."

Tenko thanked Lemba warmly, and then he turned to Birno. "Birno, I give the eagle to you and to Lokar to do with as you please. I only ask that I may have six feathers from the wings and the two claws."

Birno plucked six feathers from the wings and with his flint knife he cut off the two claws. "They are yours, Tenko. What will you do with them?"

"Three feathers I will give to Brockan to wear as a headdress." He handed them to Brockan. "The other three shall be my headdress, so that men everywhere will know we are brothers."

Brockan clasped his feathers with pride and lifted eyes full of brotherly love to Tenko.

"And the claws?" Birno asked.

"I give one to Lemba to use when he draws patterns on his clay bowls, because he has shown me friendship."

Lemba took Tenko's hand warmly. "I shall draw still better patterns with this claw."

"And the other claw?" Birno asked.

"The other claw I give to Kali to wear as a necklace, so she may never forget the day of the eagle."

Kali lifted her warm brown eyes to Tenko. For a moment they looked at each other in silence and in kindness as Kali received his gift.

4. The Day of Korwen's Revenge

Although it was late spring and the hillsides were warming to the sun, at night there was a keen air that made men seek the peat fires on their hearths. The families gathered round, sitting on stone slabs that served them for chairs. Birno's hut was the biggest, so often the Skara folk came in friendly fashion to sit round his hearth. Especially they came if Lokar was there and could be persuaded to tell them stories of their tribe. Then the children and Stempsi sat on their beds and listened too.

No one was ever idle. Their fingers were always at work. Birno was the best carver in stone on the whole island. The children searched the beach for big round pebbles for him. These he ground against other stones till they were quite round, and then he polished them with sand till they were smooth. Then, with a flint knife, he chipped pleasing patterns on them. The men of the tribe carried these round carved stones as symbols of the Sun when they went in procession to a festival at the Ring of Brodgar.

Some of the men chipped and polished stones to make axes and hammers: others shaped small pieces of bone with their flint knives to make needles and awls and pins to fasten their sheepskin cloaks. Stempsi sewed together sheepskin tunics for her family, piercing them with a fine bone needle and threading them with sinews drawn from the sheep. Kali sat cross-legged beside Brockan and Tenko, making headbands of soft lambskin. Into these she fastened the eagle's feathers. They were for Tenko and Brockan to wear when they took part in the great procession to the Ring of Brodgar. Tenko and Brockan were busy too. They were making necklaces of the teeth of sheep. They pierced a hole through the root of each tooth and threaded them together. Brockan's necklace was to be for Stempsi but Tenko's was for Kali. Only Lokar's hands were still. He sat on the biggest stone slab and peered into the fire as though he could see strange things in the flames and smoke. Now and again he turned his head to look searchingly at Tenko sitting on the bed he shared with Brockan.

"What do you see in the fire, Lokar?" Birno asked.

"Many things, Birno."

"Things that have been, Lokar, or things to come?"

"Both, my son."

The men waited for Lokar to speak: it did not do to hurry him.

"I look back into the past and I see many journeys such as Tenko has made."

The men's hands fell still. They fixed their eyes on Lokar.

"We here at Skara are herdsmen. Herdsmen we have been for as long as men can remember. Our fathers and grandfathers and their fathers before them have tended their sheep and cattle in this island of Orkney. But it was not always so." Lokar paused a moment. His eyes stared at the smoke curling lazily through the wide hole in the roof. "Once our tribe were hunters like Tenko here. We roamed great lands where trees grew."

"Trees?" Lemba lifted his eyes from the clay pot on which he was marking a diamond pattern.

"Yes, Lemba, trees. You have all seen Tenko's boat by which he came to this island?"

They nodded. There had been many visits to inspect the dugout canoe. Many hands had felt at its wood.

"In Tenko's land trees grow as the plants and bushes grow here. Their stems are thick and hard like Tenko's boat. There are so many of them that a man could get lost among them for days. Is that not true, Tenko?"

Tenko nodded. "It is indeed, Lokar. Among the trees we hunt many strange, fierce animals."

"Tell us about them, Tenko," Lokar prompted him.

"There are wolves which can tear your flesh from your bones if you are not quick enough with a bow and arrow. There are deer too with great branching horns like trees in winter."

"We have deer on the hills in Orkney too, but they are not such big ones," Lemba remarked.

"There are bears – great creatures covered in fur that can stand up like a man. They have strong arms that can crush a man if the bear catches him."

The men opened wide eyes of wonder.

"Wild boars we have too in plenty. If they charge at you they can roll you over and trample you into the ground. All these we hunt with bows and arrows," Tenko told them. "We catch fish too in our dugout boats, as big as this!" Tenko stretched his arms wide in the age-old gesture of fishermen.

"Long ago that was how our tribe got meat too, by hunting and fishing," Lokar told them. "Now we have learned to tame our animals and herd them."

"So Tenko's people are not so clever and wise as we are?" It was Tresko who spoke with a slight sneer.

Tenko bristled. He was about to speak angrily when

Kali touched his arm and put her finger to her lips. Lokar was speaking.

"I did not say that, Tresko. Each tribe has its own ways and its own wisdom. Tenko's people have special skill in hunting and fishing and they can make boats. They have new weapons too, remember! Tenko's axe can cut more keenly than any of ours."

Tresko looked sullen but said nothing. He remembered Korwen's shame.

Lokar went on, "This skill in working with strange substances found among the rocks comes from a far, far land, a land far older than Tenko's land. It lies beyond the rising sun." He pointed eastward. "Long ago our people came here in boats carved from trees. They came from a great sea nearer to the sun, a sea with warm lands round its shores. There the sun is strong and the plants grow easily. It is never cold as it is here. Always there is plenty to eat. Instead of many animals in pastures the people grow plants. From the plants they make food. It is different from our meat but it tastes good."

"I have heard that too," Tenko said quickly. "The people far to the south of my own tribe grow a plant they call corn. They pound the seeds of it in a stone basin and mix them with water. Then they shape the mixture into round flat pieces and bake it on hot stones. They call it bread. I have heard it is very good."

"And is that all they eat?" Salik wanted to know.

"Oh no, Salik. They have animals too, so they can eat both bread and meat."

"The day will come when the people of our island will eat both bread and meat too," Lokar told them. "They will make axes of bronze like Tenko's and many other things, knives, arrows and pins and ornaments for the women to wear."

"Will that be in our lifetime, Lokar?" Birno asked eagerly.

Lokar shook his head. His eyes took a faraway look. "No. Many summers and many winters must come and go before these things come to pass. But your sons' sons might know them. There will be strangers besides Tenko who will bring their skills to our island. There will be wiser men than I am then."

"No one could be wiser than you, Lokar," Birno said with love in his voice for the old man. "What should we do without your wisdom to guide us?"

"There will come a time when you will not have me, my children. Only one more Feast of the Sun shall I see with you." The old man's voice took on a note of prophecy. "And for many of you it will be the last Feast of the Sun too."

The men looked from one to another. A cold dread settled on them.

"For which of us, Lokar? For which of us?" Salik asked with foreboding in his heart.

"That I cannot tell you, Salik. Some of you will be spared." Lokar peered into the fire. "But the doom will come to Skara."

"What is this doom, Lokar?" Birno urged him.

"All that is shown to me is a cloud that comes out of the sea. That is all ... a cloud. But it is a cloud of death. Some it will take, few it will leave."

"And this place? These homes our tribe built of stone long before us and where we have lived so long ... will they perish too?" Birno sounded anguished.

"The doom that takes its people will preserve Skara long after we are dust and men have forgotten us." Lokar made the pronouncement as if he spoke in a dream. "Skara will vanish from the sight of men for many, many winters and summers and then it will stand again for all to see it as it is now."

The men stared round at the thick stone walls, the stone dresser, the stone beds and the sitting-stones they had known so long. It was as though the stones trembled in the smoke.

"These are strange words," Birno said, watching Lokar.

The old man shook himself, as if he were coming out of a dream. A shudder ran round the circle of men. For a while all sat silent, each thinking his own thoughts.

"It will be dark outside," Lemba said at last.

His words were the signal for all to rise and pick up the work they had been doing before Lokar's words shook them into stillness. One by one they took their leave. Lemba took Lokar by the arm. They went by the narrow passage that led to the paved tunnel, and went to their own homes. Birno's family crept into their beds, but Birno sat for a long time, staring soberly into the embers of the fire.

The next morning was bright and sunny. It was not their turn to herd the sheep, so Kali, Brockan and Tenko went down to the shore. Today Tenko had promised to take them along the shore in his boat. He took with him his bow and arrows.

They raced each other over the sand dunes to the white sands of the Bay of Skaill. "I'll reach the boat first!" Tenko cried.

Kali was fleet-footed and a match for Tenko, who was carrying his weapons. Neck and neck they raced, with Brockan only a yard or two behind. Almost in the same moment Kali and Tenko touched the boat together. Laughing, they both claimed the victory.

"Shall we push the boat down to the sea?" Brockan asked, eager to take his turn with the wooden paddle Tenko carried.

Tenko looked at the state of the tide. "The tide is coming in. If we wait half an hour we shall not have so far to pull the boat to launch it. While we wait, what about some target practice with the bow and arrow?" Tenko asked Brockan.

Brockan was delighted at the idea. "What shall we use for a target?" he asked eagerly. "That rock along the shore?"

Tenko looked at the rock, frowning a little. "No. It would blunt the point of my arrows. A pity there are no trees here!"

Kali had an idea. "Let us mark out a circle on the sand dune, where it slopes down to the beach."

With the point of his arrow Tenko drew several circles one inside the other on the sloping sandbank. "Now let us try it," he said and measured out a hundred paces over the sands of the bay. "We will shoot from here. I will try it first."

Slim and upright he lifted the bow to his shoulder. The arrow flew right into the heart of the target, the eagle feather fastened to the end of the shaft quivering in the sunshine.

"Tenko! That was a fine shot!" Kali cried.

"Now you, Brockan!" Tenko said.

Brockan's first shot fell wide of the circle. He clicked his teeth in annoyance. "Go on! Laugh!" he said, but Tenko did not laugh.

"Try again! Hold your bow higher and look along your arrow before you shoot. Remember all I taught you on the hillside."

Brockan tried again. This time he hit the circle, not at the centre but well within it.

"I will bring back the arrows," Kali offered.

Brockan tried his hardest and succeeded twice in hitting the centre of the ring. It was when Kali handed back one of the arrows that Tenko saw her wistful look as Brockan took his stance again.

"Would you like to try my bow and arrow too, Kali?" Tenko asked.

Kali opened her eyes wide. "But I am a girl!"

"That is no reason why you should not shoot an arrow," Tenko told her.

"Oh, Tenko, will you let me?" Kali was breathless with joy.

"Yes. Take hold like this!" Tenko instructed her as he had done Brockan.

Kali was so anxious to do well that she listened very carefully to all Tenko's instructions. She took a careful sighting along the arrow and pulled the cord as taut as it would go. Then she let the arrow fly. Straight into the circle it went, only a hand's length from the exact centre!

"Well done!" Tenko patted her shoulder. "Try it again, as many times as you like, Kali!"

Kali had the keen vision of a herd lass used to watching for straying sheep afar off. She was taller than Brockan and able to hold the bow higher. Her third shot hit the exact centre of the circle. Tenko was as pleased as if he had shot it himself.

"What did I say? There is no reason why a girl should not shoot an arrow well. You may not be able to shoot as far as a boy, for you have not as much strength in the arm, but you can shoot as straight."

Brockan had been running to and fro with the arrows for quite a time.

"Do I not get another turn to shoot?" he asked at last.

"Why, yes! You shall take it in turns," Tenko said at once. "Listen! Why should you not shoot against each other, turn about, to see who hits the circle the most times?"

The children jumped with delight at the thought of a competition.

"Right! Then I will fetch the arrows from the target," Tenko decided. "You start shooting first, Brockan."

Soon they were both aiming eagerly at the target. Both of them sent their arrows well within the circle, but although Brockan scored marks on the target, it was Kali's arrow that more often found the centre of the circle.

They were all so absorbed in what they were doing that they did not see a figure squirming through the long marram grass on the top of the sand dunes. It was a boy, who crouched low as he crept along. When he got near to the end of the sand dunes he went down on to his stomach and pulled himself along. Only a ripple in the marram grass betrayed his presence. Soon he was close to a gap in the dunes where he could peer down to the sands below. With hatred and jealousy in his heart he watched the children shooting their arrows. He saw Tenko just below him measuring the shots within the circle and retrieving the arrows. A large round pebble as big as a clenched fist lay beside him. His hand closed round it.

Kali first saw the movement among the marram grass. Brockan was shooting. The arrow fell near the centre of the target not far from Kali's last shot. Kali took the bow from Brockan. She saw Tenko stoop to measure which arrow lay nearest the bull's-eye. As he did so his back was to the sand dune upon which the lad lay hidden. The third arrow was lying at Kali's feet. She swooped on it and fitted it to her bow. The figure on the sand dune rose and stood erect. It was Korwen! He lifted his arm high to crash the stone down on Tenko's skull.

Kali let fly the arrow. It flew well and truly to its mark. It pierced Korwen's sheepskin cloak and pinned it to his right shoulder. Korwen uttered a shriek of fear and the stone dropped from his hand. Tenko sprang round and ran up the sand dune. Kali and Brockan came running too.

Korwen bellowed with pain and terror. He tried to pluck the arrow from his shoulder but the pain was too much for him. It would not come out. He was white and fainting by the time Tenko reached him.

"Keep still! Keep still!" Tenko commanded.

"Do not kill me! Do not kill me!" Korwen begged.

"Why should I kill you?" Tenko asked in contempt. "Keep still, while I see what I can do about this arrow."

"Get it out! Get it out!" Korwen shrieked frantically. "Get it out and I will never try to harm you again."

"You may be sure I shall try to get it out," Tenko told him coldly. "I value my arrow too much to leave it sticking in your skin."

Kali reached them, breathless. "Oh, Tenko, are you all right?"

"Of course! Why not!" Tenko looked surprised. "That was not a very good shot, Kali. Your arrow has never flown so wide of the circle before."

"I was not aiming at the circle. I shot at Korwen. He had that great stone in his hand ready to bring it down upon your head."

"It is a lie! It is a lie!" Korwen yelled, fearful of what Tenko might do to him.

"I believe Kali. There is the stone at your feet. And why did you beg me not to kill you? Why did you promise you would never try to harm me again! Those were your own words, Korwen," Tenko told him sternly.

"Take out the arrow and let me go," Korwen begged him, wincing with pain.

"You will say first that you are the liar and not Kali."

"I ... I am the liar," Korwen faltered abjectly. "Only take out the arrow, Tenko. Look at the blood! I shall bleed to death."

Tenko laughed. "You will not bleed to death, Korwen. It is only a flesh wound. The arrow has pinned the cloak very neatly to your shoulder. Perhaps you are not such a good shot after all, Kali. A couple of hand's-breadths and you would have pierced his throat instead." Tenko's voice was taunting, but it was not for Kali that his mocking words were meant. Korwen gave a shudder.

"I aimed at Korwen's arm," Kali said simply, annoyed that Tenko should speak slightingly of her marksmanship.

"Then you should be thankful to Kali, Korwen, that she showed you mercy and that her aim was good. When she has had more practice she will be even better. Take care you do not try to injure us again or Kali's next shot might go straight to your heart." Tenko spoke menacingly. "If her arrow does not reach it, then mine will! And now I will do something about that arrow. It will hurt you when I get it out but I will be as swift as I can. Lie down on the ground."

Korwen had no choice. Trembling, he lay down. Tenko put a foot on his opposite shoulder and grasped the protruding shaft of the arrow with both hands. He gave a strong, sharp tug. Korwen let out a shriek of pain. Tenko stood with the freed arrow in his hand.

The blood streamed from Korwen's torn shoulder.

"It is all right now, Korwen. It is out," Tenko told the fainting youth. "Down to the sea with you now and wash the wound in sea water!" He pulled Korwen to his feet and half carried, half supported him down to a pool at the water's edge. He rolled Korwen into it and Kali waded in too and splashed water over Korwen's shoulder with the clay cup she carried in her skin bag. Korwen wept with the pain and the sting of the salt water on his bleeding shoulder. Even Tenko felt sorry for him.

"It hurts, I know, but this way it will heal better. The salt water will clean the wound. You will have a sore shoulder for a few days but soon you will be able to use your arm again. You may carry the mark of the arrow for the rest of your life. Be thankful it is only a flesh wound."

"I am, Tenko! I am," Korwen cringed abjectly.

"This time you have got off lightly. You are to promise you will seek no revenge on Kali, for if you do, I will kill you as I killed the eagle." Tenko's voice was deliberate and cold.

"I promise you, Tenko! I promise! I will never touch Kali."

"Then you may go," Tenko told him. "But take care, Korwen."

Korwen departed, nursing his right arm. For a time the children sat silent, their gay spirits dashed by what had happened. Tenko looked sadly at the blood-stained arrow he held in his hand. "I am sorry this happened," he said. "I wanted to live in peace with my new tribesmen. I have seen too much of battle."

Kali knew he was thinking of his dead father. Her eyes filled with tears. "I had to shoot," she told Tenko. "If I had not done, he ... he might have killed you, Tenko."

Tenko laid a gentle hand on her arm. "I know, Kali. I know. But for your quick action ..." His voice trembled a little. "Besides, you shot to wound and not to kill. It was a fine piece of marksmanship, Kali."

"I do not think Korwen will dare to trouble us again," Brockan declared. Then, dispelling the sadness that had fallen on them, he asked briskly. "Well, are we going to push out the boat and go fishing?"

The dark spell was broken. Tenko leaped to his feet. "Look! The tide is high. Help me to haul the boat into the water."

5. The Day of the Tree

Tenko and the children smoothed the sand, moving stones and pebbles out of their path. Then they pushed the log-boat down the slope to the sea. The tree trunk was thick and heavy, but foot by foot it went down to the water. Once it was at the edge the rest was easy. The moment it floated it seemed to be a live thing. They pushed it into slightly deeper water. Tenko got in the stern and pulled the boat round by the paddle so that it faced out to sea.

"Get in!" he cried to the other two.

Kali and Brockan had brought with them improvised paddles made from the shoulder blades of an ox. With these they dipped into the water on either side of the craft. From the stern Tenko swung his wooden paddle to either side, giving a sharp twist of the blade to direct the boat.

They paddled round the bay to the north, where an outcrop of rock lifted between the sea and the sandy shore. Flatfish were often trapped in the rock pools left by a shallow channel between the outcrop and the shore.

Tenko rested his paddle and peered down into the water as the boat quietly drifted.

"There, Tenko!" Brockan's quick eyes spotted the first movement in the water below them. A plaice was trying to scurry away. It sank motionless on the bed of the channel, so that its spotted skin would make it invisible in the sand. Tenko fitted an arrow to his bow. The children watched silently. The bow twanged and the arrow cleft the water and pinned the plaice to the sand.

"Got him!" Tenko exclaimed with satisfaction. "Hold the boat steady!" He flung off his tunic and dived overboard, shattering the sunlit water into a thousand golden flashes. The sea closed over his heels. He grasped the arrow and brought the fish up impaled on the end of it. He came swimming upwards.

"There's one for our supper, Kali!" he cried, as he grasped the side of the boat. "We'll get more yet."

Tenko climbed into the boat again. Now began a competition among the three of them to be the first to spot another fish. The one who saw the fish had the right of the first shot with the bow and arrow. Kali added two haddock, Brockan a sole, while Tenko brought up three more plaice.

"That's enough, Tenko!" Kali laughed. "Another fish and there'll be no room for us in the boat!"

At last they tired of fishing with bows and arrows.

"Let us push further along the coast," Tenko suggested. "I want to see what is beyond the rocks to the north."

"Those are the rocks of Verron. There is often rough water off those rocks," Kali said doubtfully.

"If my boat would stay afloat in the storm I came through to reach your island, it will stay afloat now," Tenko said confidently.

"Maybe there will be good limpets and crabs by the rocks of Verron," Brockan said hopefully.

"Brockan, you are always thinking of your stomach," Kali laughed.

"So am I! So are all of us! Paddle your hardest!" Tenko exhorted them.

They reached the rocks of Verron and found a funnel-shaped

opening leading deep into the rocks. Along the gully ran a narrow shelf of rock. Here they were able to land. As the tide was still dropping they pulled the boat up on to the shelf.

"How shall we get it launched again?" Kali wanted to know.

"Just roll it over into the water!" Tenko laughed. "It will be a lot easier than pulling it across the beach. Then we'll dive in and swim to it."

They clambered along the rocky shelf. Brockan was quite right. There were good limpets to be had there. Soon the flint knives were out and they were chipping away. Tenko climbed further along. Suddenly he gave a shout. "Come here! There's a cave!"

The other two came as fast as they could over the slippery rocks.

"Let's explore it!" Brockan cried eagerly.

"We cannot go very far inside. It is too dark," Kali demurred.

"We'll go a little way and then wait till our eyes get used to the darkness," Tenko persuaded her.

The shallow shelf of rock continued into the cave. Peering ahead, half feeling their way with hands and feet, they pushed on step by step into the darkness. Tenko went first. The shelf was becoming narrower.

"We'll wait here till our eyes see better," Tenko suggested.

For a few minutes they stood, staring into the darkness.

"Tenko, is it quite so dark further on? I think I can see the shape of a rock ahead," Kali said.

"Let us go on a bit. Be careful, though. The ledge of rock is narrower and there is water below in the gully."

They followed in Tenko's wake, their voices echoing eerily in the cave.

"The cave bends to the left here," Tenko warned them. "Keep feeling for the cave wall."

They rounded a rock and the darkness turned to a dim twilight.

"You're right, Kali! There is light coming from above. The cave slopes upward to an opening," Tenko cried.

It was Brockan who first saw the strange thing in the water below their ledge. "Oh, look! What's that?" he cried in terror, clutching at Tenko. "What is that dark thing, waving terrible arms? Is it a spirit of the cave come to snatch us?"

He turned to run and would have fallen into the water below if Tenko had not grabbed him. Tenko's heart had leaped and thudded for a second, but he saw that the object did not move any nearer to them. All at once he knew what it was.

"Stay here!" he said to the other two. "I am going to have a closer look."

"No, no, Tenko!" Kali implored him. "It might seize you!"

"I do not think it will. If it is what I hope, it will do us no harm."

Tenko drew his bronze axe from the deep pocket of his deerskin tunic and held it ready. Though the arms of the thing swayed a little in the moving water they were not extended to grab him. Tenko crouched down, crawling nearer and nearer to it as he would creep up on an enemy. One of its arms was outstretched towards him. Suddenly Tenko dealt it a blow with his axe. There was a splintering sound but the arm did not move. Tenko stood up and gave a cry of joy.

"Come here! Come here!" he shouted. "It is what I thought."

Kali and Brockan came slowly, timidly, not quite sure of their safety.

"What is it, Tenko?" Kali whispered. Even her low voice echoed mysteriously round the cave.

"It is a tree!" Tenko shouted triumphantly.

They drew closer, staring.

"But trees do not grow on our island. Even bushes would not grow in a cave." Kali's voice was incredulous.

"I did not say it was growing. It is a tree, though, a dead tree."

"But how would it have got in here?" Brockan asked.

"It must have come from some other land, perhaps even my old land. It has been uprooted in a storm and the wind and the waves have brought it here, just as they brought me. It must have been washed into this cave and become wedged at the end of it. Now we shall have to try to get it out again."

"Get it out?" Kali was astonished.

"Yes. It would be foolishness to leave it here. We can use the trunk to make a small boat. We could use the branches too and with the strong twigs I can make more bows and shape arrows too."

Kali and Brockan saw the sense of this at once. "Another boat? Perhaps for me!" Brockan thought, boy-like.

They bent down and tugged with Tenko. The tree moved about a foot and then it stuck. Not all their efforts would dislodge it.

"It is wedged in some crack in the rocks below the water," Tenko decided. "I am going into the water to find out what is holding it."

"Into that dark water? Oh, Tenko!" Kali feared for him.

"Do not be afraid. I shall be all right, Kali."

Tenko lowered himself into the gully. First his knees were covered by the water. He took a step forward and sank to his waist. Another step and he was up to his armpits, but a fourth step took him into water up to his waist again.

"It is not too deep for me." He took a deep breath and stooped, thrusting his head and shoulders under the cold water. He felt about with his hands and then rose, gasping but triumphant.

"I've found it! Only one branch as thick as my arm is wedged between two rocks. That is what is holding the tree."

"How will you get it loose?" Brockan asked. "Shall I come in the water beside you to help?"

"No. You stay where you are. You and Kali tug gently at the branches. I'm going to cut off the branch that is wedged."

It took Tenko a number of shallow dives and blows with his axe before the branch was severed. The tree responded at once by rising higher on the surface of the water. Kali and Brockan grabbed at it to prevent it floating away down the cave. Tenko emerged from the water, clutching his axe. He climbed up on to the ledge beside them.

"Now to haul it down the cave to the gully mouth," he said. "Whatever happens, we must not let the tide take it away from us."

"How can we get it out?" Kali asked. "If we lean over the rock and pull it we shall overbalance."

"Yes, that is true." Tenko considered for a moment. "The pull of the falling tide is strong. The tree will float down the gully of itself but it might get wedged behind another rock. It might even get swept out to sea and then we should lose it for ever. There is nothing for it but for me to go into the water and hold on behind it."

Kali looked at Tenko fearfully. "What if you got caught in the branches and drowned?"

"Not I! I will hang on behind the tree and hold on to its torn roots. I can always let go if the tree is too much for me."

"How can we help, then?" Kali asked.

"I will go with the tree as far as the bend in the cave and try to lodge it against the rock there. That is quite near to where we left the boat. Can you and Brockan manage to roll the boat down into the water?"

"Yes, we can do that."

"Then I'll swim in close and grab it. Try to keep up with me as I drift down the cave with the tree but watch your step in the darkness. Hang on to the tree now till I get hold of its root. Kali, will you take care of my axe?"

Kali received the axe and laid it carefully beside her on the ledge. The two children held on to the tree by the branches which rose above the level of the path. Cautiously Tenko let himself down into the water again. He grasped the broken-off, trailing roots of the tree.

"Now let go!" he shouted to the children. "Give the tree a push away from the side."

The tree began slowly bobbing along the water on its course down the gully to the open sea, Tenko floating behind it, a grey shadow on the dark water. Kali picked up Tenko's axe and held it tightly to her. The two children worked their way along the path, watching their footing and keeping alongside Tenko and the tree. Now and again the tree caught in a rock and Tenko had to tug it backwards and forwards. Once he had to call to Kali, "Hand me my axe! The tree has got wedged again."

Kali knelt on the edge of the rocky path and leaned forward as far as she dared without overbalancing. Tenko swam close in to the rock and stretched out his hand to take the axe. The water had fallen lower than when they had entered the cave and Tenko's reach was a foot too short.

"Drop the axe and I'll catch it," Tenko directed her. Kali hesitated. The sharp edge of the axe might wound Tenko's hand if he caught it by that. If the axe slipped his grasp it might be lost in a deep hole in the gully for ever. She knew what store Tenko set by his axe. Still clutching the axe tightly she slipped over the ledge and into the water beside Tenko.

"Oh, Kali, why did you do that?" Tenko cried.

"Here is your axe." She thrust it at him. "It will need one of us to hold on to the tree when you release it with your axe or it might float away too quickly."

"I could swim after it."

"You would be cumbered then by your axe and have only one hand free. Now there are two of us to hang on to the tree." She shouted up to Brockan, "You will be all right by yourself, Brockan?"

"Yes, I'm all right. I'll make my way to the boat."

Kali held on tightly to the tree root while Tenko swam round the tree to find the branch which had caught. It was difficult to locate in the darkness. At last he found it. It was a forked branch which had stuck in a cleft in the rocks. Luckily it was a very slim branch, no thicker than Tenko's wrist. With a couple of blows he severed it from the tree. At once the tree began to move downstream again, but this time with Kali pulling backwards on its roots. Tenko took his place beside her, grasping another root with his free hand. Brockan shadowed them along the ledge.

At last they reached the place where the cave took a sharp bend. Here they could see the sky at the end of the cave and the gully where the boat was lying on the ledge. On the point of rock at the sharp bend there were one or two larger rocks lying out in the stream.

"Steer the tree over to those rocks," Tenko directed Kali.

They got the tree lodged behind the rocks. The weight of the falling tide held the tree against them.

"It will be safe here," Tenko said. "We can climb out now over the rocks to the ledge again and get to the boat."

The seaweed-covered rocks were very slippery. Kali found it hard to get a grip and pull herself over them. More than once she slipped and Tenko grabbed her. Then they came to a rock below the ledge. It was sheer on the side facing the water. The top of it was beyond their reach!

"Hold on to the rock and I will see if it is easier lower down the gully. Can you keep my axe?"

Tenko climbed carefully down again. Kali held on to a tangle of seaweed and waited in the half darkness. Then, handhold over handhold, his feet feeling for clefts in the rock, Tenko came up beside her again.

"No, the rocks are sheer above the water lower down the gully too. There is only one way to the ledge, Kali. We must go back to the tree."

It was a nightmare journey over the slippery rocks, but Tenko took it slowly, steadying Kali now and again. Brockan called out to them, fear in his voice. "Are you all right? What is wrong?"

"We are coming, Brockan. We are finding a way up." Tenko tried to make his voice reassuring.

They slipped down into the water again. It felt colder than ever. They had to fight hard against the downward surge of the tide to reach the tree. They held on to it, panting to get their breath back. Tenko climbed up the half submerged trunk till he reached the branches. Now began the really tricky part of his climb. The branches were wet and slimy. One or two of them were rotten from submersion in the sea water. Tenko tested each branch with his hands before he trusted his weight to it. Once there was an ominous cracking. Kali, below, cried out in fear.

"It's all right, Kali. A small branch broke but I grabbed another," Tenko called to her.

At last he reached the stout branch that overhung the ledge of rock. Like a monkey he curled his arms and legs round it and then twisted his body till he was on top of the branch. His training as a hunter had taught him how to climb trees. He crawled along the branch till he was able to let his feet down on the ledge.

"It is not difficult to reach the ledge, Kali. I'll come back and guide you up the tree," he called to her.

Kali still held Tenko's axe. He had forgotten all about it in his fight to reach the ledge. Kali would have only one hand free unless she left the precious axe behind. She made a quick decision.

"No, Tenko. It will be quicker if you join Brockan and launch the boat, then you can come and fetch me. I ... I do not think I could climb over the branches as you did."

"It might be better to fetch the boat," Tenko agreed. "Can you hang on to the tree?"

"Yes," Kali replied, though her voice trembled a little. "Be as quick as you can, though. It's cold in the water."

Tenko rounded the bend and hurried along the widening ledge as fast as he dare go on that slippery surface towards Brockan and the boat.

Kali got a grip of the tree trunk with her free hand and threw a leg astride it. She managed to pull herself on to the trunk. Little by little she edged her way along it till she was free of the water. That was better. The bitter-cold water no longer surged about her. It was eerie, sitting in the cave with only a glimmering of twilight about her. Every sound, the rushing water, the snapping of twigs, echoed and re-echoed in the cave. There was always a strange murmuring. Kali tried to keep from thinking of the stories her tribe told of the spirits of the sea and the spirits of the caves; of the strange creatures that came up out of the sea to grab their prey. She gripped the tree trunk, as much petrified by terror as by cold.

Tenko reached Brockan, who was standing by the boat.

"First we must take out the bow and arrows and put them where we can reach them easily afterwards from the boat," Tenko said.

"There is a place lower down the gully where the rock shelves into steps. I have been looking already," Brockan told him.

"Good! Take them and put them out of reach of the waves. Take Kali's paddle too."

By the time Brockan returned Tenko had the log-boat poised on the edge of the rock, ready to roll into the water below.

"We shall have to leap in quickly after the boat before the tide carries it away. Keep a tight hold of your paddle and grab the boat with your free hand. I'll do the same. Are you ready? Then over with the boat!"

The boat rolled off the edge and hit the water with a mighty splash. Tenko did not wait for the boat to reach the water before he plunged in after it. Immediately the boat began to float downstream. Tenko was after it like a swift fish. The current helped him. He grasped the stern with one hand and pushed it in towards the rocky wall of the gully. There the tide held it for one brief minute, but it was long enough for Tenko to throw his paddle aboard and heave himself after it. With the paddle he thrust vigorously and brought the craft up to the wall and held it there. Another moment and Brockan was swimming alongside. Tenko stretched out a hand and hauled him into the boat.

"Well done, Brockan! Now we must paddle against the current to get back to the tree and Kali. It will take all our strength."

Tenko pushed out a short distance into the stream. Together they thrust their paddles as hard as they could but they seemed to make little headway against the outward rush of the tide. Time and again Tenko had to pull in to the side and hold on to a pinnacle of rock while they got their breath. Then, all at once, the force of water seemed to slacken. The thrust of the current was not so strong against them.

"The tide is turning!" Tenko cried with joy. "Now we shall have slack water for a short time. Paddle hard to get up the cave, Brockan."

It was tricky work manoeuvring the log-boat among the rocks at the turn of the tide. There were sudden whirlpools that set the boat spinning and rocks that seemed to heave themselves up in mid-channel. Foot by foot, they fought their way along. As soon as they reached the bend in the gully Tenko called out, "Hold on, Kali. We're coming!"

Kali heard them with thankfulness. Her hands and feet were growing numb, but she never relaxed her grip on the bronze axe. At last Tenko and Brockan appeared like grey ghosts out of the twilight. Tenko brought the boat alongside the tree as near in as he could get for the branches. He managed to wedge it between two rocks.

"Can you get along the branches to the boat, Kali? Wait! I will come to help you. You hold the boat where it is, Brockan."

He climbed cat-like along the branch nearest to Kali.

"Give me your hand, Kali."

"First take your axe and put it safely in the boat," Kali said in a faint voice.

"My axe! I had forgotten it!" Tenko exclaimed. "I was thinking of you and not of the axe, Kali."

Tenko's words sent a warm feeling to Kali's heart. "All the same, take it first," she told him.

He climbed back to the boat with it, and then returned and gave Kali a hand over the branches. At last she was safe in the boat. Now came the difficult business of freeing the tree again from the rocks and bringing it alongside the boat.

"How can we fasten it to the boat?" Brockan wondered.

"By the bow-cords and all our leather girdles," Tenko decided at once. "We will tie them to the branches. You, Kali and Brockan, will sit in the stern of the boat and hold on to the leather thongs and tow the tree after the boat. I will do the paddling."

"What if the tree comes crashing on to the boat?" Kali asked.

"I do not think that will happen. The incoming tide will hold it back and its branches will catch the rocks and prevent it moving as fast as the boat. You must be careful it does not pull you overboard."

Tenko secured the thongs to the tree branches and passed the ends to Kali and Brockan. Then he jerked the tree away from the wedging rocks. The rising tide helped to float it. It would have drifted up into the cave again but for the pull on the leather thongs. Kali and Brockan held on tightly. Tenko seized the paddle and plied it for all he was worth. It was hard work now against the incoming tide, but the deepening water in the gully prevented the tree from catching on the bottom. At last they reached the mouth of the gully and the open sea. All three heaved a sigh of relief. They pulled alongside the rocky ledges and while Kali and Tenko held the boat there with their hands, Brockan sped up the step-like rocks to fetch back the bow and arrows.

Now they had to head out into the open water. It was difficult battling against the incoming waves and keeping the boat head on to them with the tree acting like an awkward tail at the end.

"Shall we never reach the point of the rocks where we can turn in towards the Bay of Skaill?" Tenko panted, his breath cutting his chest like a knife.

At last they were well clear of the treacherous rocks. Tenko turned the boat and rested for a minute or two and drifted with the tide. Then once more he seized his paddle and thrust hard with it. The sea and the wind helped him, but it also brought the tree fast after them. Kali and Brockan had the double task of hanging on to the thongs and constantly fending off the tree from the boat. At times it seemed as if the tree would overwhelm the boat.

Tenko had an inspiration. "Hold on tightly, both of you! Let the tree drift alongside. Move up the boat with it but do not stand up or you might overbalance. Shuffle along as you sit. Do it very slowly now."

Kali and Brockan obeyed him. Little by little they edged the tree round till it was alongside. Tenko was right. Now the tree helped to tow them. Tenko thrust his paddle into the water again. "Now for Skara!" he cried in triumph.

The folk of Skara were on the sand dunes watching them come in. Stempsi had been anxious when her family had not returned by midday and had gone in search of them. Korwen told her he had seen them heading out to sea. When the sun began to sink Birno and the stoneworkers returned. The whole settlement became uneasy and gathered on the dunes and scanned the horizon to the north-west.

At last they saw the small specks of the tree and log-boat against the setting sun. They grew larger. Now they could distinguish the three figures in the boat.

"They are all there!" Stempsi cried with relief.

"What is that thing they are bringing with the boat?" Birno asked, puzzled.

Lokar knew. "It is a tree!" he cried gladly. "The boy from the sea is bringing a tree to us."

The boat headed for the shore and the folk of Skara ran down the beach to meet it. As soon as the log-boat grounded,

Tenko and the children leaped ashore. With the help of the villagers they hauled the tree up the beach. Lokar went to meet them.

"I have brought you a tree, Lokar!" Tenko cried. "It has drifted to our shores from some far land. Out of it we can make another boat and hafts for your axes and many other things. I give it to you, Lokar, for the people of Skara, because I am one of you now. The boat we shall make from it shall be for all the people of Skara to use."

Lokar put a hand on his head. "You have done well, Tenko."

"I could not have done it alone," Tenko said quickly. "Kali and Brockan helped me."

"Kali and Brockan, the tribe owes you thanks too. As for you, Tenko, you have proved yourself a true son of Skara."

A shout of acclamation rose from the crowd.

6. The Day of the Whale

The next day the men of Skara stripped the branches from the tree. They worked with their flint knives, hacking away, while Tenko's bronze axe flashed in the sun. They took the branches to Lokar's hut, where they would be safe until they could be shaped for use.

"How are we going to make a boat of this big trunk, Tenko?" Birno asked. "It is going to take us many a moon to hollow it out with our knives."

"There is a quicker way than that," Tenko told him. "First, it is true, you must do a little hollowing out with your knives. But afterwards we use fire."

"Fire?" Birno asked.

"Yes, when we have hollowed out a shallow groove, then we will bring peats from the fire and set them in the hollow and leave them to burn."

"But will they not burn away the whole tree?" Lemba asked anxiously.

"No. We must watch it till it has burned deeply enough. We will have bowls of sea water at hand to throw upon the fire and put it out when the hollow is deep enough for men to sit in."

They chipped away with their flint knives, working through all the hours of daylight. In three days Tenko thought the hollow was deep enough. On their bone shovels they carried smouldering peats and packed them loosely in the hollow carved in the tree and left them to burn away. Day and night a man in turn watched to make sure the fire did not go out nor yet burn too fast. Tenko constantly inspected it.

"It is ready now," he pronounced at last when almost the whole centre of the trunk had been burned away, leaving a thick shell of wood all round it. They dowsed the fire till only a mess of steaming charcoal was left in the hollow.

"As soon as it is cool enough, you must get to work with your knives again," Tenko said.

It was much easier to chip away the burned wood in the hollow. With flint knives and adzes made of stone the men cleaned and deepened the centre of the craft.

"It will drive more easily over the waves if you shape the ends to a point," Tenko directed. Once more the men worked on the boat until Tenko declared it was ready for the water. Then they shaped paddles out of some of the thicker branches. Tenko took the supple thick twigs which would easily bend to make bows. Others he shaped into arrows.

At last came the launching of the boat. The men pushed it into the sea and watched anxiously while Tenko tried it out. He made a wide circle round the bay and came back to the anxious group on the beach.

"It is good," he said with satisfaction. "The Skara boat goes well. I should like Birno to be the first to try it."

Birno eagerly climbed in and took the paddle. Tenko gave the boat a push into deeper water. At first Birno wobbled slightly till he learned to adjust his balance.

"Take care, Birno! Remember the boat is rounded and can easily turn over in the water," Tenko shouted to him.

Soon Birno got the knack of handling it and brought the Skara boat triumphantly round the bay. Lemba did well too. Salik had his turn too, but he did not venture so far and soon brought the boat back again.

"I think I am made for a herdsman and not a fisherman," he said. "All the time my stomach was turning over inside me."

Tresko sneered at him. "You are soon scared, Salik. I will take my turn with the boat now."

Birno looked questioningly at Tenko, but Tenko nodded. He gave Birno a grin.

Tresko seated himself in the boat and seized the paddle.

"Watch me!" he cried.

He moved into the bay at a good speed and seemed to be doing quite well. Tenko, however, stepped into his own boat and said to Birno, "Take the other paddle, Birno. We will go after Tresko. I doubt if he can really handle the boat."

Tenko's boat with two men in it moved faster than the Skara boat. They began to make up on Tresko. Tresko turned his head and saw them rapidly approaching. He decided to show them he could easily keep ahead of them. That was his undoing! He failed to steer towards the oncoming waves, but turned beam on to them. It seemed as if a playful wave was waiting. It rolled the log-boat over and Tresko fell into the water with a shriek. When Tenko and Birno caught up with him, Tresko was hanging on to the capsised boat.

Tenko brought his own boat alongside. Tresko grasped it with the grip of one half drowning.

"Do not hang on to the side, Tresko! You might overturn us too. Work your way towards the stern of the boat," Tenko told him.

Tresko paid no heed.

"Come on, now! Do you want me to bring my paddle down on your hands?" Birno cried. "If you upset us we shall be so busy saving ourselves that we shall have no time for you."

Reluctantly Tresko shifted his grip a hand at a time till he had worked his way to the stern.

"Pull me into the boat!" he cried.

"No! You must hang on and be pulled through the water," Tenko told him. "Birno, can you manage the boat alone?"

"Why? What are you going to do?" Birno asked in alarm.

"Swim after the other boat! Already it is drifting away. We are not going to lose it after all our trouble in making it. I must take my paddle in case I cannot recover Tresko's. Steady the boat while I jump!"

Tenko stood up and leaped lightly into the water. Pushing the paddle before him, he swam after the other craft.

"Are you not making for the shore?" Tresko asked Birno. "It is very cold in the water."

"Kick your legs if you are cold," Birno told him in a contemptuous voice. "I will wait to make sure Tenko is safe."

Tenko reached the Skara boat. He held his paddle between his knees so that he had both hands free. Then, reaching under the craft, he gripped the boat and gave a heave to it. It turned over and began to ride the waves right side up. Tenko took hold of his paddle again and swam after the boat. He flung the paddle aboard and then pulled himself into the craft by the stern. He picked up the paddle and turned the Skara boat towards the shore.

"It's all right, Birno! Let's go!" he called.

Birno started paddling too. Both boats moved towards the shore with Tresko trailing like some strange fish behind the bigger craft. Willing hands pulled their boats ashore when they reached shallow water. Tenko leaped out and went to aid Tresko up the beach. Tresko looked half-drowned, frightened and utterly miserable. All his conceit had vanished. It would be a long time before he would venture out in the craft again. Korwen came towards him.

"Look after him, Korwen. He'll feel sick," Tenko advised

him. He turned to Birno. "I could not find the paddle. It had floated away."

"Then we must make another." Birno sounded vexed. "We will make it a rule that if any man loses a paddle, he must carve another."

"Yes, but the wood will not last for ever. The shoulder blades of an ox are not nearly so easy to use," Tenko reminded him.

The men of Skara learned to use their new boat, all except Tresko, who had had enough of it. Birno and Brockan proved specially skilful at handling it. Besides making arrows out of the spare wood, Tenko made a long spear out of a straight branch and wedged a sharp flint arrowhead at the top of it. This was useful for fishing for flatfish in the shallow water and for poking crabs out of their holes. The fish made a welcome change to their main diet of beef, mutton and limpets.

One day Birno was in the smaller Skara boat while Brockan and Kali were with Tenko in the larger boat. As they pulled across the Bay of Skaill, Brockan suddenly pointed with his finger into the water below them. The tide was nearly full. A great shoal of whitebait like a silver cloud was moving in a solid mass towards the shore.

"What is happening?" Brockan cried.

The children rested their paddles and Birno pulled alongside them. The whitebait did not seem to notice the splash of his paddle or the shadow of his boat above them. The great wedge of fish drove on frantically.

"There is something strange going on in the water," Tenko said.

"Look what is coming after them!" Kali cried.

It seemed as if the oncoming waves were made of silver. The sea was a seething mass of shining herring.

"Are they chasing the whitebait?" Kali asked.

The herring moved in a jostling, heaving mass, forced on by some panic. They drove on towards the land.

"Some enemy must be chasing them!" Tenko cried. "They are trying to get away from something that is pursuing them. What is it?" He stared out to sea. Beyond the herring shoals, moving lazily into the Bay of Skaill, was a low dark shape, curving slightly against the horizon. "Look! Look over there!" Tenko pointed.

"What is it?" asked Kali, frightened.

"It is a great fish, greater than any I have ever seen," Birno said.

Tenko's face was alight with excitement. "It is a whale!" he cried. "It chases the herring shoals."

"A whale? Lokar once told us about a whale." Birno began to get excited too. "Long ago there was one came ashore in Orkney, long before our time, near one of the other tribes. It could not get back into the sea and it died on the beach. The great fish had red flesh like beef. The folk of the island had plenty of meat from it. The fish had great bones too, so big that folk used them in building their houses. If only this whale would come ashore in the Bay of Skaill, we could use it!"

"Then we will drive the great fish ashore," Tenko decided.

"Tenko! It is so big that with one flip of its tail it could turn our boats over and smash them to pieces," Birno told him.

The whale was swimming in much closer.

"If we could frighten it into a panic, like the other fish, then it might come right into the bay. The tide is near the turn. It might get left behind on the beach," Tenko said.

"If we frighten it, it is more likely to turn and make off into deep water again," Birno pointed out.

"Then we must get in behind it, so that we are between it and the deep sea," Tenko cried.

"That might be dangerous," Birno said.

"There might be time to take Kali and Brockan back to the shore first ..." Tenko began.

"I don't want to go back!" Brockan declared, his blood afire at the thought of the adventure.

Kali stiffened. "I will not go back either. I'll go with you, Tenko."

"You are sure, Kali? You are not afraid?"

"I am sure." Kali's lips set in a determined line.

"Are you willing, Birno?" Tenko asked.

"Yes, I will follow you, Tenko."

"Then pull as fast and as hard as you can to the south to get round the whale."

They pulled south till they were well clear of the shoals of fleeing herring and then came about again and turned north. The whale was still chasing the herring to the shore, gulping down mouthfuls of them. He was unaware of the danger coming to him from the sea.

"We will wait till the tide is turning," Tenko decided. So much depended on choosing the right moment to close in on the whale. If he struck too soon the whale might get away to the open sea again. The whale was still intent on the herring. The silver fish jostled and fought to get further inshore from him.

"It is slack water now. We will close in till we are within arrow-shot of the whale," Tenko directed them. "Do not splash with your paddles. We must do nothing to frighten him till we are ready."

Dipping their paddles gently into the water they went after the whale. He still moved inshore, but the water was getting shallower under him. They drew closer.

"Good! He is moving towards the reef. If we can force him just over the rocks ... Steady the boat for me!"

Kali and Brockan put out steadying paddles. Tenko fitted a sharp barbed arrow of bone to his bow. Birno watched him and did the same with a flint-topped arrow.

"When I rise, you do the same, Birno. Steady your boat and then let fly when I say 'Now!'" Tenko directed. "Brockan, will you and Kali be ready with your bows and arrows as soon as I have shot mine?"

The children nodded, breathing fast with excitement.

Tenko rose in one swift movement. Birno stood up too. His boat wobbled a little but he soon got it balanced again.

"Ready, Birno?" Tenko whispered.

They took sights along their arrows at the bulk of the whale just ahead of them.

"Now!"

The bows twanged. The arrows flew straight. The barbs penetrated the skin and well into the flesh of the whale and stuck there, quivering. The whale jumped as the arrows stung him and he leaped into the air. He came down with a flop on the water, which made their boats rock. Tenko quickly steadied his craft.

"Now, you, Kali and Brockan!"

With two paddles outspread Tenko balanced the boat. Kali and Brockan took aim. Two more arrows pierced the whale's skin.

Now the great fish was aware he was being attacked. He threshed about with his tail, churning up the water. The canoes swung this way and that.

"We must get in even nearer," Tenko said, wielding his paddle furiously. For a minute the whale remained still. Tenko and Birno used that minute to fit two more arrows to their bows. Then they rose swiftly and let fly.

This time the arrows penetrated deeper and blood began

to pour from the small wounds they had inflicted on the whale. Suddenly the whale turned to face his attackers. This was the most perilous moment. Tenko was ready for it with another sharp barbed arrow fitted to his bow. "Steady now!" he yelled to the children.

The whale charged towards Birno's boat. In that instant Tenko let fly. The barb struck the whale just inside his tiny eye and lodged there. The rush of the whale halted. Terrified, he swung round. He plunged and thrashed in an effort to dislodge Tenko's last arrow. The sea boiled round the log-boats. Tenko managed to keep his larger boat from overturning, but Birno's boat rolled over. He gave a yell as he found himself in the seething water.

"Oh, Father! Father!" Kali cried in terror.

Birno surfaced in a moment. He was a powerful swimmer and in a few strokes he reached his boat again. He managed to right it and climb in, but he had lost bow and arrows and paddle. Tenko had quickly brought his boat round to rescue Birno. The paddle went floating past Tenko's boat. Kali reached out an arm and grabbed it.

"Well done, Kali!" Tenko cried. "Are you all right, Birno?"

"Look! The whale!" Brockan yelled.

Tenko swung round, thinking the whale was coming to the attack again. The whale, however, had been seized by the panic which had affected the herring. He only wanted to get away from his attackers. He was heading blindly for the shore.

"After him! After him! The tide has turned!" Tenko cried. "We mustn't let him turn back now."

Kali passed Birno his paddle and the two boats sped after the whale. Once again they were within shooting distance. Tenko and Brockan both shot again, Kali steadying their boat. The arrows lodged in the whale's tail. Terrified, he took a leap towards the land. His leap took him over a reef of rocks below the water.

"We've got him! He can't get away from there easily," Tenko yelled, excited. "Follow him up!"

The whale had realised his danger and turned to head out to sea once more. The boats reached the reef. Tenko shot one more arrow, this time at the other eye. Never had he shot so well! The blinded whale turned again, not knowing which way he was headed. He flopped in the shallowing water over the reef and into a pool at the other side. Then, blowing out his breath in a column of vapour, he gulped in air again and sank down into the pool.

"The water will run quickly out of that pool. It will not be long before he finds himself on the sand," Tenko said.

True enough, the great whale felt his body touch the bottom of the pool. He gave another leap to try to get back into the sea but slipped off the jagged teeth of the rock back into the pool again. He turned in panic and gave a convulsive leap in the opposite direction. He found himself lying on the shingle beach. He tried to edge himself backwards into the water again, but a barbed arrow poked into his flesh. Spent and breathing hard, he lay on the shingle. The water in the pool grew less. Every minute he lay there, he had less chance of getting back into the sea.

Tenko and Birno brought their boats over the shallow water on the reef and into the quieter channel on the other side. The whale gave a flip of his tail but could not move his great bulk more than an inch or two. His huge body was his own undoing. His great weight was meant to be supported by the sea. As he lay on the beach the bulk of his flesh was pressed against his lungs. He could not breathe properly. He tried to raise himself on his paddle-like flippers but sank to the sand again. Slowly his own weight suffocated him. His struggles grew feebler.

"He is nearly finished," Tenko said.

Tenko and Birno took their boats to the edge of the pool now well below the whale. The tide was running out fast. A knot of the Skara people had gathered on the shore. They had watched Tenko and Birno pursue the whale. Now they waited for the whale's end to come.

The whale's breath came shallower and faster. There was a little pause for a few moments and then the breathing would start up again. The pauses became longer. The whale was dying. He could only live if he could get back to deep water and that was now impossible. The folk of Skara watched and waited.

At last the great whale lay quite still. There were no more whistling breaths. Not a tremor came from a flipper. Tenko leaped from his boat to the sandy bank of the pool. "Wait!" he shouted to the others.

With bated breath Kali watched him approach the whale. Tenko took out the bronze axe from the deep pocket inside his tunic where he always carried it. He stood beside the whale for a moment, looking at it. He seemed so small beside the great shape. The folk on shore stood as if turned to stone as they kept their eyes on him. There was stillness and silence everywhere. Tenko raised his axe. He brought it crashing down on the blunt forehead of the whale. Blood gushed from the gash, but no movement came from the whale. He was dead indeed. Tenko gave a shout of triumph.

It was as though Tenko's shout released everyone from a spell. Birno and the children leaped from their boats. The people from Skara came running along the beach. They gathered round the whale, shouting for joy. Lokar came, hanging on to Lemba's arm.

"Well done, Tenko, my son! Well done, Birno! We watched you from the dunes as you chased the great creature ashore. What will you have done with it now?"

"There is meat here for the tribe for many days," Tenko told him. "The great bones can be used for many things, for weapons and for tools."

Tribal memories stirred in Lokar. "From the fat of the whale there comes oil. Oil will burn with a flame that will give us light in our dwellings on dark winter nights."

Tenko gave a glance at the sea. "Come, people, out with your axes and knives. Let every man take away as much flesh as he can carry for himself and his family. You must work quickly before the tide rises again and floats away the whale."

Tenko mounted on the slippery body of the whale and began hacking away with his axe. The men of the tribe came with their stone axes and flint knives and began tearing at the whale's flesh.

"Why, it is red like the flesh of cattle!" they cried in surprise. All the fish they had known had white flesh. Here was a creature of the sea with flesh like that of their own animals!

There was a thick layer of fat underneath the skin. This the men stripped off. The women carried it away in their big earthenware bowls. From all points of the compass screaming gulls and gannets descended on the shore, brought there by the sight and smell of the meat. The children were set to scare them away. The men tore at the red flesh. There was a terrible pandemonium what with the shouts of the men, the yelling of the children and the screaming of the seabirds.

Blood ran everywhere. The arms and tunics of the men were soaked in it as they hacked at the carcass and staggered with great lumps of meat to the dunes. The air was thick with the stench of blubber and whale meat. The women built peat

fires in the hollows of the dunes to smoke the pieces of meat, so that they could be rubbed with salt and preserved for a time in stone chambers under the ground. The folk of Skara did not even pause to eat. Eating could be done later. Now they had to save their precious booty from the grasp of the sea. They worked away feverishly.

When twilight came the tide was returning. The fires still burned and the smell of roasted whale meat filled the air. The gulls were still screaming and darting in to seize pieces of meat. Most of the flesh had been stripped off the whale. The bony skeleton was left with scraps of meat still adhering to it.

"The bones are light enough for us to pull out of the reach of the sea," Birno decided. "Bring leather thongs from your houses."

The men knotted the thongs together to make reins. Each man harnessed himself to the reins by a loop tied in the thongs. Even boys like Brockan joined the teams of men. The leather reins were tied to the whale's skeleton. When all was ready Birno gave the word.

"Pull!" he shouted.

The men heaved on the leather reins. The skeleton of the whale came slowly up out of the hollow in the sand it had made for itself. When it was halfway up the shingle they paused to get their breath and ease their aching muscles. The tide was beginning to run rapidly over the sand.

"Pull again!" Birno cried.

With chests almost bursting with effort they strained again at the leather thongs. The women left the children to keep the marauding birds off the meat. Headed by Stempsi, they came down to help the men. Stempsi organised them into a team to push at the skeleton while the men heaved. Foot by foot, yard by yard, they brought the great framework of whalebone to the foot of the dunes, where it was among dry sand and pebbles and out of the reach of the tide.

"It is all right now," Birno shouted from his place at the forefront of the men. "We can let the seabirds have it now. They will pick the bones clean for us."

Hardly had they loosed the leather thongs from it and staggered away than the seabirds descended in a cloud upon the remains of the whale.

That night at Skara a great feast was held. Never had there been so much meat to eat. Tenko's and Birno's names were spoken with gratitude. Birno and his family ate well too, but Tenko remembered that a hunter should never eat too much or he might become too slow. The men ate and ate and slept, but not Tenko. Outside it was moonlight. Tenko stepped over the snoring men and along the passages to the huts. From her stone bunk Kali saw him go. Like a shadow she rose and followed him. At the entrance to the village she called, "Wait for me, Tenko!"

Tenko turned at her voice and waited till she caught up with him.

"Where are you going, Tenko?" Her voice trembled a little.

"Just to look at the whale."

"You were not ... not going away in your boat?"

"Why, no!" Tenko was surprised.

In the moonlight tears of relief gleamed in Kali's eyes.

"Why, Kali, what is the matter?" Tenko asked.

"Promise me you will never leave the island unless you take me with you," Kali entreated earnestly.

Tenko did not reply at once. "Come with me to look at the whale," he said. "I will answer you then."

They ran barefoot over the grassy dunes. There before them was the great skeleton of the whale, picked clean now by the beaks of seabirds and gleaming white in the moonlight. They slowed down as they came up to it. Tenko laid his hand upon the framework of the ribs.

"Kali, a hunter cannot stay for ever in one place. I am not a herdsman like the folk of Skara. My people move from forest to forest, from shore to shore. It was as Lokar told you. Once both our peoples came from a great land and a great sea far away towards the midday sun. We have always taken journeys. Some day the call will come to me to go and I shall have to answer it."

"I know! I know!" There was a sob in Kali's voice.

"But this I promise you, Kali. By the bones of this great whale we have hunted together I swear I will take you with me wherever I go."

Kali gave a long fluttering sigh of relief. "And Brockan?" she asked.

"Brockan shall come too if he wishes. He is my brother."

"We are your brother and sister always," Kali said.

Tenko looked long at Kali in the moonlight. "You are my sister now, Kali, but you may not always be my sister."

"I do not understand."

"It is not the time yet for understanding," Tenko said with a wisdom beyond his years. "That day is not yet. Now let us go back to the hut where they sleep."

7. The Festival of the Sun

With their stone axes and Tenko with his bronze axe, the men of Skara broke up the skeleton of the whale. Each man was given a share of the whalebone. Lokar saw that all was done fairly.

"As Birno and Tenko, Kali and Brockan brought the whale to our shore, to them should go the bones they choose."

"I choose the two jawbones," Birno decided. "With them I will make rafters for the thatch of my roof."

"And you, Tenko?" Lokar asked.

"I will take some of the smaller bones to make harpoons and enough of the whale's teeth to make a necklace."

Brockan chose a bone that he could shape into a large knife.

When Kali's turn came she pointed to the whale's backbone.

"Those bones could be used for little dishes to hold paint when the men paint their bodies for the Festival of the Sun. I should like some small bones too that I could shape into bone pins for our cloaks."

Some of the men used the ribs of the whale to make supports for their roofs; the women rejoiced over bone to make needles to sew their sheepskin garments. Even the children were given large flakes of bone to work into knives. The tribe felt richer than it had been for many years.

The summer days grew longer. The sea sparkled round the islands, fringing the edges of the shore with curling white.

On the cliffs the seabirds fed their young. The gannets dived after fish, the terns wheeled over the sea, giving their plaintive, wailing cries, the black shag quarrelled among themselves as they stood in rows on the rocky ledges. The hills sloped greenly to their rocky summits and on the lower slopes the flocks of the tribe grazed.

It was drawing near Midsummer day. There was hardly any night at all in Orkney. By the Point of Howana the sun plunged into the sea to appear again three hours later over the shoulder of the Hill of Cruaday. As each night became shorter, excitement grew in the tribe of Skara. Soon there would be the Festival of the Sun, when the tribesmen of Orkney met on the rising hill of Brodgar between the two great lakes. There, in the circle of giant stones, at midday on the longest day, the men would make a sacrifice to the Sun God.

The women prepared new tunics of the softest sheepskin. With flint scrapers they scraped away the wool and washed the skins in the stream that ran from the Loch of Skaill. They kneaded and pounded them on the stones till the skins were soft and supple. Then they shaped them into tunics, sewing up the sides with sinews from the sheep. Kali joined the women in their work. She had begged two soft lambskins from Salik and these she worked on till they were soft as the lambswool itself. Kali sewed them into a tunic, but she was not content with that. She bored holes in sheeps' teeth she had collected and sewed them round the neck of the garment in a pattern. She tacked a deep pocket on the inside of the tunic and fastened it with whalebone pins. When it was finished she took it to Tenko.

"This is a new tunic for you to wear at the Festival of the Sun. Your deerskin is stained by salt water and torn by the rocks."

Tenko looked at the tunic with delight. For a moment he

was speechless. Then he stammered, "You ... you made this for me, Kali?"

"Yes, the womenfolk of Skara always make new tunics for the men of their families when they walk in procession at the Festival of the Sun," Kali told him. "My mother has made a new tunic for my father and one for Brockan. I made this one for you, Tenko."

Tenko put out a hand and stroked the soft skins. "I have never had such a beautiful tunic," he declared. He fingered the bead-like pattern. "But you, Kali ... What will you wear at the Festival of the Sun? Should not this tunic be for you?"

Kali shook her head. "The women do not walk in the procession. We follow after the men in a crowd. No woman is allowed within the Ring of Brodgar, so we watch from the outside. We wear what necklaces we possess. I shall wear the eagle's claw you gave me. No one else will have an eagle's claw," she said proudly.

Tenko suddenly dipped into the deep pocket of his old tunic where he always kept his bronze axe.

"I have been making something for you too, Kali." He pulled out a necklace. It was made of the teeth of many animals, beautifully polished and shining white. They were graded from the very small teeth of rabbits and lambs to the larger teeth of sheep and cows. There were nearly a hundred of these ivory beads and from the centre hung two of the great teeth of the killer whale they had forced ashore.

Kali exclaimed in delight, "Oh, Tenko! Not a woman of my tribe has such a fine necklace!"

"Put it on," Tenko said to her. "I will fasten it behind your neck for you." Carefully he tied the sheep's sinew on which the beads were threaded into a firm knot.

Kali knelt and looked at her reflection in a still shallow sea-pool. She drew in her breath sharply.

"Oh, Tenko! The necklace is so beautiful! I will wear it always. It shall never leave me, waking or sleeping."

Tenko looked more than pleased.

From behind a rock Korwen had watched the exchange of gifts. His face grew dark with hatred and jealousy. He sought out Tresko and told him what he had seen.

"The stranger from the sea will have a finer tunic than any of us," he said.

Tresko sat chewing his nails for a few minutes and then he laughed shortly.

"Tenko may wear his new tunic with pride, but he will not wear it for long. He will be sorry that men look twice at him when he walks in the procession. I have thoughts in my head that I will keep till the day of the Festival of the Sun. Be content till then, Korwen."

In preparation for the longest day of the year the tribe of Skara had many things to do. The previous day they cast off their old tunics and rushed into the sea. They rubbed their bodies with white sand till the skin was reddened. This was the ceremony of cleansing.

Next came the ceremony of painting. The women had prepared pigments in little basins made from the vertebrae of the whale. There was a yellow paint made from a clay ochre, a red paint made by crushing pieces of rusty-looking rock, and blue paint from a flax plant.

The men dipped wads of sheep's wool into these paints and rubbed them over their faces and bodies, making bold patterns. Tenko watched Birno, not knowing what to do.

"Come, Tenko! Smear on the red paint." Birno offered him the wad.

Tenko shook his head. "In the forest we did not paint ourselves. The smell of the paint would give us away to the animals."

"Did you not even paint yourselves in honour of the Festival of the Sun?" Birno asked.

"The men painted themselves only if they went to war with another tribe. That was to make them look more frightening. Also it showed to which tribe they belonged. Here on the island you do not go to battle, do you?"

Birno shook his head. "Not now! We all live in our own villages and look after our own flocks. Their meat gives us enough to eat. We have no need to fight, so we live in peace."

Tenko considered Birno's words gravely. "I think that is a good thing, that you live in peace."

"You said your tribe of hunters painted themselves to show to which tribe they belonged?"

"Yes."

"We too make a sign on our chests to show we belong to the tribe of Skara. See this!" Birno opened his tunic. Upon his chest was daubed a round red circle. "It is the mark of the Sun God. All our people carry it. If you do not wish to paint the rest of your body, Tenko, will you bear this mark to show that you belong to our tribe? I ask you to do this because you are now my son."

"Because you ask it, Birno, I will bear your mark on my chest," Tenko told him.

Birno gave Tenko a little cup of the red paint and a swab of the wool. Tenko left the rest of the men and climbed over the rocky reef. When he was out of sight he opened his tunic and painted the sign of the sun upon his chest. He sat looking out to sea till the paint was dry, and then he drew his tunic about him and went back to the rest of the tribe.

The women had been busy in the houses. They had roasted

great joints of beef and mutton and wrapped them in the leaves of plants and put them in skin bags. The waterskins had been filled at the spring. The women polished their necklaces of bone beads and combed their long hair with bone combs till it lay straight and sleek. Now all was ready for the morning and they lay down to sleep.

At sunrise the people of Skara rose. In Birno's hut Stempsi was astir first. She and Kali went to milk their cows. They returned with the bowls of milk and Stempsi set them to heat on the glowing peats. There would be no meat eaten till after the Festival of the Sun. This was a law of the tribesmen. Except for a drink of milk they must come fasting to the meeting place at Brodgar. Some tribes came many miles from the east and south of the island. They made the journey the day before and camped for the night near the narrow neck of land that ran between the two great lakes of Stenness and Harray. There the tribe from Skara would join them.

Stempsi laid ready the new tunics that she and Kali had made.

"Today Tenko will wear the new tunic I have made for him," Kali said with pride.

Stempsi gave a little sigh. "May it bring him joy and not misfortune."

Kali caught at her mother's hand. "How could a tunic bring him misfortune?"

"I do not know. Think no more of it, child. They were stupid words that came from my mouth. Come, let us wake the others." Stempsi lost the strange look that had come into her eyes and spoke briskly. All the same, Kali looked troubled. It was said among the tribe that Stempsi had "the sight," the gift of seeing into the future that her grandfather Lokar possessed.

The menfolk donned their new garments and in a moment

Kali's fears were forgotten. Birno looked striking in his red, blue and yellow paint. Brockan was wearing his plume of eagle's feathers. So was Tenko. He stood erect in the fine new tunic with its pattern of gleaming white teeth. Kali felt proud to see him wearing her handiwork.

"Come! Drink your milk!" Stempsi called to them. Into the big bowl they each dipped a smaller bowl and drank.

In all the stone houses of Skara the same thing was happening. The folk drank their bowl of milk and then made their way to the meeting place in the village. Lokar was there already, his staff in his hand, seated on a large stone. He was saving his strength till all the tribe assembled. Although they had less than seven miles to walk to the ring of Brodgar, it was a long way for an old man whose limbs were becoming feeble. Besides that, once they had reached the ring, Lokar would have to stand for some hours.

At last the tribe was assembled, old and young. Birno came to the meeting place carrying six beautifully carved stone balls. These were the symbols of the sun belonging to the tribe of Skara. Some of them had been carved by men of the tribe long since dead, but two of them had been carved by Birno himself. Birno looked with pride at the last stone ball he had carved. The carving on it was so deep that the pattern stood out in spikes like a hedgehog. It had taken Birno a whole year to carve, sitting by his fire at nights. The spikes represented the rays of the sun. He carried the symbols to the waiting crowd.

Birno handed the oldest sign of the sun to Lokar. It was a beautiful pebble that had been chipped and polished to a perfect sphere. He handed another to Lemba the potter; the third to Salik the herdsman. Over the fourth Birno hesitated. Tresko set him with his glittering dark eyes as though daring

Birno to refuse to give him one of the symbols. Birno recognised the seething hatred in Tresko. He would do nothing to placate him. Instead he turned and handed the stone ball to a young man, Ramna.

"You have worked hard at the quarrying, Ramna. This is your reward."

Ramna held the engraved ball high above his head in a gesture of worship to the sun. Tresko's frown deepened, but there were still two symbols left in Birno's hands. Birno turned to Tenko.

"I give this sign of the sun to Tenko to carry in the procession," he announced in a loud voice. "He has done many things for our tribe. He killed the eagle which raided our flocks, he made us a tree-boat and he brought the whale to our shores."

There were shouts of approval from the tribe, but Tresko stood aloof, glowering. "He is not one of the tribe of Skara," he objected.

"He is one of the tribe because I have taken him for my son. Remember, Tresko, that as head of the tribe of Skara I have the right to say who shall carry the signs of the sun at the midsummer festival," Birno rebuked Tresko.

Tresko's frown deepened, but he said no more.

"Are we ready now?" Birno asked briskly. "Take my arm, Lokar, and we will lead the way."

They went by the Loch of Skaill and then along a sheep trail over the slightly rising ground. They passed a quarry in the side of the low hill. Birno pointed to it.

"That is the quarry of Bookan. That is where I split off the great stone for the Ring of Brodgar. From here we dragged it with ropes of hide to the ring of stones. That is the stone we are going to raise today," he told Tenko with pride.

The land narrowed. On either side they could see the placid waters of two great lakes, Stenness and Harray. The long neck of land between them was holy land to the tribes of Orkney. On a mound rose the temple they were building to the sun. The gaunt slabs looked immense and awe-inspiring, outlined against the sky. As they approached the circle the men of Skara stopped as one man and they looked up at it with reverence.

The Ring of Brodgar was to be a circle of giant stones when it was finished. These stones were slabs of solid rock about ten feet high and over a foot thick. Their bases were buried deep in holes in the ground. Their tops had been split in a diagonal line that seemed to make them point to the sky.

"There are only twenty stones standing yet. When the Ring of Brodgar is finished there will be sixty stones," Birno explained to Tenko. "It takes many moons to hew and shape a stone in the quarry and to drag it to Brodgar. I have been working in the quarry all my life and I have set up only four of the stones. Today the fifth stone is ready and we shall hoist it into its place. It is good that we should do this at the Festival of the Sun. After that we shall make our sacrifice and then we shall all eat together, the people of Orkney."

Tresko was listening. At the word sacrifice his eyes glittered unpleasantly.

The ring of stones was surrounded by a deep ditch thirty feet wide, partly filled with water.

"It took many years for the men of Orkney to dig this ditch. They laboured hard from dawn till sunset and grew old and bent with the work," Lokar told them. "It was told me by my father and his father before him, and so for many generations. Yet not a man grudged giving his health and strength in the service of the sun."

There were two ways across the moat directly facing each

other, one at the north-west and one at the south-east. In these places the earth had been banked up to make a road twelve feet wide. At the north-west crossing Birno halted and lined up his people. Only the men would cross into the sacred ring. The women stayed on the far side of the moat. They would watch everything from there. When Birno had formed the procession to his liking he gave the word, "Lift up your symbols of the sun!"

The six leaders held the carved stone balls high in their hands. Some strange compulsion made Tenko take his bronze axe from his pocket and lift it high in the air too. It flashed brightly in the sunshine. Tresko scowled at him. Even Birno looked at him inquiringly.

"Why do you do that, Tenko?"

"Because this axe is the sign of the people from whom I came, who also worship the Sun. You are kin to us because our speech is almost the same. I have vowed this axe to the service of my new tribe."

"It is good," Lokar said approvingly. "That axe is the sign of things to come, of a new way of life. The Ring of Brodgar belongs to the past and to the future too. Let Tenko carry his axe proudly."

"It shall be as you say, Lokar. Men of Skara, let us go into the ring," Birno gave his command.

The company advanced across the earthen bridge with the signs of the sun held aloft. Tenko's bronze axe flashed fire when the sun's rays caught it. Silently they joined the procession streaming from the south-east. Three times the tribes of Orkney marched round the Ring of Brodgar and each time the men passed the highest stone of all, they lifted the signs of the sun which they carried and shouted loudly. Tenko waved his bronze axe and shouted too.

The march over, the great work of erecting the new stone began. It lay on the ground, one end of it close to a deep hole ready to receive it. There was a sloping channel hollowed out towards the hole. The other end of the stone pointed out towards the moat. Between it and the moat was a rough platform of slabs of stone. On one end of this platform rested a longer thinner stone with its end chiselled and sharpened. This was the giant lever.

Men came running from every tribe, carrying long ropes of cowhide, knotted and strong. Two men dug with bone shovels and scraped away the hearth in a hollow just below the outward end of the stone. When the hollow was deep enough the men with the cowhide ropes slipped their nooses round the pointed end of the great stone. There were six long ropes: three to pull the stone upward, and three stretching in the opposite direction to steady the stone from toppling over once it had slipped into the hole and was standing erect. Teams of men from all the tribes manned the ropes. Six of the strongest men mounted the stone platform. Birno climbed up with them. It was his duty to oversee the work and to shout commands. The six men seized the lever stone and thrust the pointed end into the hollow below the stone that was to be hoisted in the ring. All eyes were on Birno.

"Heave!" he cried to the men at the stone lever. They pressed their weight down on their end of the lever.

"Pull!" he shouted to the men on the far ropes. At once they began to haul. The men on Birno's side of the stone held their ropes slackly. They would be ready to take the strain of the stone's weight when Birno gave the word.

The great stone was levered upward a few inches. The men on the ropes opposite pulled with might and main. Slowly the end of the giant stone began to rise. When it was about two feet in the air Birno called out, "Halt! Hold fast, everyone! Do not let go, but do not pull."

It was necessary to lower the stone platform so that the men could get the lever at a sharper angle. A big stone wedge was placed to hold the lever in position. Stones were lifted from the platform. This was a tricky business, for the men holding the lever had to step down to a lower level and yet keep the lever from sliding. They were all experienced in handling the lever and there was no mishap. The lowered platform gave them greater leverage.

"Heave! Pull!" Birno cried again, watching both teams levering and hauling. Under Birno's commands they worked in rhythm together, so that the thrust and haul happened at the same moment. It was perfect timing. With each effort the outward end of the great stone rose higher. All at once the stone seemed to move backward of its own accord. The end of it on the ground was sliding into the funnel-like opening of the hole. As it slipped in, it became upright. This was the most difficult part of the operation; Birno had been waiting for this moment.

"Pull on your ropes! Take the strain!" he called sharply to the team on the slack ropes. When the great stone began to settle into its hole there was always the danger that if the pull on it by the first rope team was too strong it might topple over backwards. The moment the end of the stone fell into the hole there must be an equal pull on the ropes in both directions to keep it upright. The men tightened their grip on all the ropes.

"Now!" Birno cried as the end of the stone dropped into the bottom of the hole with a thud and the stone rose upwards. It wobbled dangerously for a moment but the ropes tightened on both sides and held it steady. It settled into the hole and remained erect. A shout of joy broke from all the men.

"Keep hold of the ropes. Keep a gentle pull on them. Do not let go yet!" Birno cried as the cheering died down. The men obeyed, keeping an equal strain on both sides of the stone. With bone shovels other men lifted earth and gravel and packed it tightly round the base of the stone in the hole. They tramped it down till the whole socket was solid and firm. Birno went up to the stone and tried to push it in either direction. It did not move an inch. It was as though it had grown out of the ground like a tree.

"It is good!" Birno pronounced. "The great stone stands of itself. Let go the hold on your ropes!"

Cheering broke out afresh among the men of Orkney. Kali watched her father with pride, but her glance kept turning to Tenko. He had taken his place on the rope and hauled with the rest. He had obeyed Birno's commands with joy. At this moment of achievement he felt that he indeed belonged to the tribe of Skara.

"It is well done, my sons! The Circle of Brodgar grows each year," Lokar spoke with satisfaction. "Today is a great Festival of the Sun. Our temple will one day be complete, like those temples in far-off lands of which our forefathers have told us. All our tribes are children of the sun wherever those temples are built. By the ring of standing stones shall we be known. Let us now lift our arms in the chant to the sun and then we will eat."

There came an unexpected interruption from Tresko. "Should we not make the sacrifice first, Lokar, the blood sacrifice? The sacrifice will make the God of the Sun pleased with us."

Lokar was annoyed that Tresko should interrupt. "Tresko, I will order matters in my own way."

"But in times past we have always made the sacrifice before we ate," Tresko persisted. "Let us not depart from custom, lest the Sun God be angry."

The tribe of Skara was silent. They did not trust Tresko. They knew he was sly. Birno muttered under his breath. The tribes from the east of the island, however, sided with Tresko.

"Yes, let us first make the sacrifice as we always do. Let the sacrifice be made, Lokar!" they shouted.

Lokar saw that most of the people wished to make a sacrifice. Though he was not pleased, yet he must give them his consent. The blood of a lamb from the flock must be shed to satisfy them.

"Very well! Make ready the sacrifice," he told them.

A long slab of thin stone like a table top was carried into the ring.

"Have you a lamb for the sacrifice?" asked Lokar.

"There is a lamb here, Lokar," spoke one of the chiefs of the eastern tribes.

"Let it be brought forward," Lokar commanded.

Tresko spoke again. "Wait! This year the sacrifice should be greater than a lamb. The God of the Sun has shown us favour. Our flocks have grown. We have never gone hungry. We have set up the greatest stone that has ever been brought to the Ring of Brodgar."

"True! It is true!" the crowd echoed about him.

"Then we should make a special sacrifice this year," Tresko told them.

"Yes, yes! There should be a special sacrifice," the people cried.

Lokar looked angrily at Tresko and once again took the matter into his own hands. "Which of you has a calf or cow he can spare from his herd?"

The tribesmen looked from one to another. "We have not brought our herds with us, Lokar, as you well know," one chieftain said.

Before Lokar could reply, Tresko spoke again. His voice was crafty, persuasive. "Perhaps the Sun God does not want a calf or cow. This time the God of the Sun demands the blood of one of us here present."

"No! No!" Lokar cried at once. "The Sun God does not ask for the blood of men. Our tribes have never sacrificed a man for longer than anyone can remember."

"But once our people used to do that. You have told us so yourself, Lokar," Tresko reminded him.

"Which of you would be prepared to give himself as a sacrifice?" Lokar challenged the crowd.

The people shifted about uneasily on their feet, but no man came forward.

"You see, Tresko? To take a man by force from any tribe would destroy the peace that has been among us for many years," Lokar told him.

Tresko was not silenced. "There is no need to take any man of the tribes of Orkney, so there is no need to disturb our peace. We should seek one who is not painted as we are for the Festival, who does not carry the mark of the tribe of Skara." He pointed to Tenko. "There he is! The boy with the shining axe who came out of the sea!"

"No! No!" Lokar cried, aghast at the suggestion. Birno gave Tresko a threatening look.

"Yes, yes! He is not one of us. He will do for the sacrifice," cried a chieftain from the eastern tribes. They were relieved in their minds that none of their people was to be chosen for sacrifice.

"Sacrifice the stranger! Sacrifice the stranger!" the cry rose from them. It grew and grew, echoing from one tribe to another.

Tenko stood as if turned to stone, his face pale. He knew he was in greater danger than ever before in his life and he could do nothing. If the tribes went mad with bloodlust he would be killed on the stone of sacrifice. Lokar stood between him and the excited crowd.

"No! This lad should not be killed. He has brought good and not ill to the tribe of Skara. He has destroyed our enemies in the sky and the sea. He brings us new ways of life from our kinsmen in lands over the sea."

Birno took his place alongside Lokar.

"This boy belongs now to my family. He has been accepted by the tribe of Skara. Whoever lays a finger on him will have to deal with me first," Birno declared.

The shouts of the other tribes sank to an uneasy murmur. Tresko, however, was not finished.

"If he has been accepted by the tribe of Skara, why then does he not carry the marks of the tribe in paint as we do? He is a stranger and strangers should die!"

Birno swung Tenko round to face the crowd. He pulled open Tenko's tunic and displayed the sign of the sun painted on Tenko's chest.

"There is the mark of the Sun God. There is the sign of Skara!" he shouted. "This boy is one of us. Kill him and you will answer to me for it." He swung round to Tresko. "Blood shall be answered by blood, Tresko!"

Tresko quailed before him and drew back afraid.

An angry defeated murmur rose from the crowds. The tribe of Skara made threatening gestures towards the tribes from the east who demanded the sacrifice of Tenko. They waved their fists at Tresko. Lokar knew it would take little

to set them fighting one against the other and then the Sun God would have his blood sacrifice indeed. He held up his hand for silence.

"Be quiet, my people!" he commanded. "Remember you stand within the sacred ring of the Sun." He cast a look up at the sky. Lokar's great dignity was impressive indeed. One by one the men of Orkney fell silent. There was a stillness in the Ring of Brodgar like the hush before a storm.

Lokar spoke. "This boy belongs to the tribe of Skara. You have heard what Birno said and you have seen the mark of the tribe of Skara on the boy's chest. If you men of the south and east and north kill him, then the men of Skara will seek revenge. If you break the laws of all our tribes then you will bring war upon us. The peace that has dwelt among us for so many years will be broken. Evil will sweep over the land." Lokar raised his arm impressively. "The God of the Sun who speaks to you through me demands obedience and not sacrifice. He will have peace and not war. If you disobey, the Sun God will hide his face from you. He will speak to you in a terrible voice." Even as Lokar spoke a dark cloud drifted over the face of the sun. The crowd felt the shadow sweep over them and shifted uneasily. From out of the cloud came a flash of lightning and the sudden sharp crack of thunder. The men of Orkney flung themselves on their faces. Only Lokar remained erect, his arm pointing upwards.

"The Sun God has spoken. He will have no sacrifice. He commands that there shall be peace among you. He will show his anger to the one who raises his hand against another man. Rise now to your feet. Each chief will give the hand of friendship to Birno, the Chief of Skara, who has erected the great stone for us here today. Then we will sing the chant to the sun."

One by one the painted chiefs came forward and took Birno by the hand. Many of them spoke to Tenko too. Tresko hid himself, skulking behind the men of Skara. When all had saluted Birno the tribes stood waiting for Lokar's signal. He raised his arms towards the sun. Birno broke into the chant with his powerful voice and all the people sang. Across the moat the wives and families joined in too. Kali sang with all her heart, the tears of relief that Tenko was spared rolling down her face.

"Now go to your families and eat," Lokar commanded.

The men of Orkney crossed the earthen bridges to their families. They stepped lightly, as though a burden of fear had fallen from their shoulders. Only Lokar knew how narrowly war had been prevented among the tribes. In all his days as priest of the sun there had been peace. Now the crisis was over he felt empty and drained of strength. It was with difficulty he controlled the trembling of his limbs.

"Let me put my hand on your shoulder, Tenko," he said, "I am a feeble old man."

"No, no, you are not!" Birno told him. "Who but you could have held the tribes by your will? There was strength indeed." He took Lokar by the arm. "You need food like the rest of us."

Lokar leaned on Birno and Tenko. Slowly he made his way back to the place where the tribe of Skara had assembled. Out of respect for the wise old priest they had waited to eat. Birno led him to a large stone that served as a seat.

"Stempsi has food for you. I will go and bring it," he said.

As Birno passed Tresko he stopped. "Do not think that your wickedness will go unpunished. Some day, Tresko, you will go too far. Remember this! If you so much as lay a finger on Tenko you will have to reckon with me."

Tresko shrank back and said nothing.

Tenko brought water in his bowl for Lokar from a nearby spring. Lokar drank the water thankfully. As he handed back the bowl he said, "Sit beside me, Tenko. I have something to say to you."

Tenko sat at his feet.

"There will come a time, Tenko, when I shall be no longer with you. That time may not be far off. I wish you to make a promise to me."

"Yes, Lokar."

"No matter how sorely you are provoked you will never plunge my people into shedding blood."

"I promise that, Lokar. Before I would do that I would take my boat and go back across the sea."

Lokar shook his head. "You must not do that either, Tenko." The old man's eyes gazed afar off, as though he were looking at something Tenko could not see. "There will come a time of sorrow and disaster to the tribe of Skara. Then they will look to you for help. You must not fail them."

"I will not fail them, Lokar," Tenko told him steadfastly.

8. The Day of the Fog

When the excitement of the Festival of the Sun had died down Tenko grew restless. Life at Skara seemed quiet and uneventful. Tresko and Korwen kept out of his way. The children helped with the flocks and herds. They took the boats out to the rocky reefs and brought back limpets and crabs and flatfish. In the long summer nights they sat on the sand dunes round the village and worked on bone ornaments and stone axes.

One day Kali found Tenko sitting moodily on a sand hill just above the Bay of Skaill. He was staring hard at the two boats.

"What is wrong, Tenko?" Kali asked.

"Nothing ever seems to happen at Skara. I might as well be a cow or a sheep."

Kali looked alarmed. "Do not say things like that, Tenko. Why were you looking so hard at the boats?" In her heart she was fearful that Tenko might take his boat and leave them. She did not know of his promise to Lokar.

"I was thinking of a way they could be made safer. Sometimes they roll over in heavy seas."

Kali felt relieved that that was all that was in Tenko's mind.

Tenko went on, "Listen, Kali! At the Festival of the Sun I talked with men of other tribes. One of them was a man from the north who had taken over a day's journey to reach Brodgar. He told me there were other islands to the north ... many islands. I should like to see those islands."

"I knew there was something troubling you," Kali said unhappily.

"There is always something in me that will not let me be still, Kali. Always I want to find out what lies beyond the next headland – over the next hill. But I want you and Brockan to come with me and find out too."

It was as though a stone was lifted from Kali's heart when she knew that Tenko had no thought of leaving them behind.

"The large boat will not take three of us very fast if we have to carry meat and water for a journey. The smaller one is apt to roll and it would be hard for either you or Brockan to handle it in the open sea. I have been thinking of a way to make the boats safer."

"How, Tenko?"

"There are still three small branches left from the tree we found. I am going to cut three notches in the side of each boat as they face each other. Then I am going to shape a notch like this at the end of each branch." Tenko drew a T-shaped notch in the sand. "I shall fit the notches on the branches into the notches on the boats, and the branches will link the boats together."

"I understand. It is a good plan." Kali clapped her hands.

"Then, over the three branches we can stretch a sheepskin tightly. It will serve to hold the branches in position and make a platform by which we can pass from one boat to the other. Will you help me with it, Kali?"

"Yes, yes. You know I will."

"Come now! Let us start work on it at once. We will bring the branches from my bed where I have been keeping them safe."

Kali hesitated. "Tenko, we ought to ask our father for permission to make this journey."

Tenko frowned. He did not wish anything to stand in the way of his adventure, but he knew that what Kali said was right. He thought hard for a minute. "Very well," he said at last. "I will ask Birno and Lokar. If they are willing, then that is enough."

Kali and Brockan went with him to Birno and Lokar. When Tenko outlined his plan Birno looked doubtful. "These are dangerous seas, Tenko, and the shores are bounded by rocky cliffs. You would be voyaging along unknown coasts."

"That is true, Birno. I promise you that I will not venture too far. I will go no further than two days' journey. I want to see what is beyond the headlands to the north."

"Why do you want to go, Tenko?" Lokar asked.

"There is a restlessness in me, Lokar. It comes on me like a sickness. It is as if I am seeking for something I have not found. I must see what lies behind the mountain, beyond the headland."

Lokar turned to Birno. "Our people came from far lands, Birno. It took them many thousands of moons, many generations of men, to reach this island. But always in them was the urge to find new lands. Maybe here in Skara we have grown too contented. Tenko, Kali and Brockan are our people of the future. Let them go on their adventure. It might be that Skara could vanish in a night and our tribes need new lands."

"Skara vanish in a night! Our strong stone dwellings disappear like a puff of smoke? Come, Lokar, that is not possible." Birno laughed.

"Do not laugh, Birno."

A strange uneasiness fell on them. Tenko broke the silence.

"May I take the boats and go then, Birno? Have Kali and Brockan your leave to come with me?"

"Very well, Tenko. But you are to take no risks, remember! No chasing strange monsters in the sea!"

"I promise that, Birno."

"And you will be back in the Bay of Skaill by sunset on the second day?"

"I will try to do that, Birno."

Lokar added a word of warning. "If you meet strange tribes be friendly towards them but do not trust them too much."

"I will heed what you say, Lokar."

They started work at once on the boats. Birno sometimes lent a hand with the work too. He also made extra paddles for them.

"We all know how easy it is to lose paddles," he said.

At last the boats were united by the wooden struts and the sheepskin. Tenko had made the first catamaran to sail the northern sea. He was thrilled with his achievement and bounced up and down in the smaller boat.

"Look, Birno! It will not sink! It would even be hard for the waves to overturn it. It will be difficult to steer, perhaps, but we shall soon get the knack of it."

All that afternoon they practised paddling the boats round the Bay of Skaill. Birno, too, tried his hand. "It is a good craft," he said. "It does not rock and roll in the waves."

"I shall handle the smaller boat. Kali and Brockan can take the larger one. My stronger paddling will make up for theirs and help to steer the craft," Tenko planned.

The next day was a fine, still day with no wind. The sun rose early in the north-east, a red ball of fire. Tenko and the children were up at sunrise and packed the sheepskin bags with the meat Stempsi had cooked for them. She added a small bowl of wild honey. This was a treasure indeed. It was not often a nest of wild bees was found and it was not easy to smoke them out and get the honey. Birno took six hollow horns of cattle out of his keeping-place behind his bed. These were precious possessions too.

"You can carry water in these. Fill the horns with water and tie a sheepskin over the end of each one. That will keep the water from spilling out."

"That is how the men long before us carried water on their journeys," Lokar said. "Remember to fill the drinking horns again whenever you touch land."

At last they were ready for their adventure. They pushed their craft into shallow water and got into the boats. Birno, Lokar and Stempsi watched them go, Stempsi with misgiving at her heart.

As though he could read her mind Lokar said, "Have no fear, Stempsi. This is a voyage Tenko must make for the sake of the people of Skara."

The strange craft carrying the children grew less and less in size. They watched till it rounded the Point of Verron.

All that morning the children dug into the sea with their paddles and the catamaran moved steadily northwards, helped by a gentle south-west breeze. Now and again Tenko ordered them to rest and they laid their paddles on the floors of the boats and relaxed. The urge of the tide drifted them northward. Though Tenko followed the shore he took care to keep the craft well out beyond the ground swell near to the cliffs. It was a cruel rocky shore of great headlands fringed by jagged reefs. The sun mounted higher in the sky and the children grew hungry and thirsty. Still Tenko pulled on, looking for a break in the chain of cliffs. A great headland towered to an immense height above the water. Tenko began to think he might have to turn back. Kali was flagging in her stroke on the paddle and Brockan had a blister on his hand. Then, all at once, as they rounded a sharp reef they came on a small sandy bay. A stream of water flowed down between the green hills and spread itself in shallows at the head of the bay.

"This is the place where we will rest and eat," Tenko decided.

He swung on his paddle and pulled the craft round. The two boats headed between the reefs into the bay. They leaped out when the water grew shallow and pulled the catamaran well up the beach beyond the high-tide mark. They flung themselves down on a grassy dune, glad to rest.

Tenko was the first to recover. He went down to the boats and brought back three water-horns and a skin bag of meat.

"Sit up and eat," he told the children. "You will feel better after food." He handed a mutton bone covered with meat to each of them and took one for himself. They tore at the meat with their strong teeth and drank from the horns. For a while they were too busy eating to talk.

"We will rest till the shadow of that rock reaches the pool," Tenko decided. "Then we will fill our horns at the stream and pull out into the bay again. How is your blistered hand, Brockan?"

Brockan was a tough young lad. "It does not hurt so much now."

"Let me see," Kali demanded.

The blister was red and angry-looking. She knew Brockan would suffer in silence and say nothing.

"We must do something for that, Brockan, or else you will have to give up using your paddle." She seized the soft sheepskin bag in which they had carried the meat. "Is the edge of your axe sharp, Tenko?"

"I always keep it sharp." Tenko took out the axe.

"Hold it with the edge upwards, Tenko." Kali took the bag and holding the edges of it tightly she pulled the bag over the sharp edge of the axe till it split. Turning the bag this way and that she managed to cut a square of soft supple skin.

"Give me your hand, Brockan."

She fitted the sheepskin round his hand like a fingerless mitten, leaving the thumb free. Then, with the bone needle she usually carried and a thread of sinew, she sewed the mitten over Brockan's hand and secured it at the wrist by sinews fastened round it.

"Is that comfortable?" she asked Brockan.

"Yes. Much better."

Kali looked about her. There was a soft green moss on a rock. Kali knew this moss had healing properties. She gathered some and went back to Brockan. "Tuck this inside your palm over the blister. It will make a soft pad inside the covering."

Brockan was comforted and relieved. "I shall be able to wield the paddle all right now." He did not wish to fail Tenko on this voyage that meant so much to him.

"We will fill the horns again at that stream and then we will push on further," Tenko directed.

They followed the stream inland for a short distance till they came to another stream running into it. Here the water tasted fresh and free from salt.

"Drink your fill while you are here," Tenko advised. "That will save the water in the horns to drink when we are on the sea."

When they had refilled the drinking horns they went back to the catamaran and pulled it down into the water. To the north were towering cliffs.

"Will you still pull north, Tenko?" There was an edge of doubt in Kali's voice.

"I want to see what is beyond that headland, Kali. Perhaps we shall come to the islands of which I was told."

Kali knew that when Tenko had set his mind to a thing there was no turning back for him. Silently she took up her paddle and they struck out for the north-west.

Tenko guided the craft well out beyond the flurries of white where the waves dashed at the foot of the headland. They looked up at the towering red sandstone ledges above them. They were the nesting places of thousands of screaming seabirds, gulls, guillemots and razorbills. The children watched them plunging and diving into the sea after fish, and carrying back their catch to the clamouring nestlings.

They bent to their paddles again and rounded the headland. The sheer cliffs bent away to the north-east. For an hour they paddled, talking little, saving their energy for their strokes. To the north the reefs curved in a menacing bow. Did the reefs end in an island? Tenko thought he saw green slopes shining in the sun. "Could this be the first of the islands that lie to the north?" he cried.

A cloud floated between them and the sun. The warm shimmer left the water and the sea became a menacing grey. Kali shivered. She cast a glance towards Tenko's island.

"Tenko! I cannot see the island as plainly as when you first pointed it out," she said in an anxious voice.

"You will see it when the sun comes from behind the cloud," Tenko said confidently.

But when the sun came from behind the cloud the island was blotted out. It had vanished completely.

"There is a sea mist rolling down upon us," Kali said with misgiving at her heart.

Already the line of reefs to the north had become hazy. Out to sea a white mist shrouded the horizon. There was a wet cold feel in the air.

"Will you turn back?" Kali asked.

"No. To get round the headland we should have to pull far out to sea. If this sea fog surrounded us we might have no notion which way we were going. We might pull further and further out to sea. The water in the horns will not last for ever. We do not want to be lost out of sight of land and die of thirst."

"But you can hardly see the land now," Kali cried in dismay. "We might be dashed upon those reefs."

"We will take the chance of that," Tenko decided. "At least if I cannot see the land I can hear it."

"What do you mean?"

"Tenko means he can hear the waves dashing against the reefs if we move closer in," said Brockan.

"But how will that help us?" Kali asked.

"When the waves beat upon a sandy bay they sound different from the terrible crashing they make on the rocks. We will nose our way along slowly, listening all the time till I hear waves upon sand. That will mean there is a break in the rocks. We will steer for the break and try to run the boat on to the beach."

Tenko sounded so calm that Kali was reassured. They turned the catamaran eastward nearer the land. Though the sea mist closed round them, they could still see a few yards in all directions.

Tenko kept a sharp lookout. The fog seemed to press on his eyeballs and dance in a hundred flickering points of light. He listened all the time. The children kept taking a few strokes with their paddles and then stopping and listening. The sea was calm, but gradually the crashing, grinding noise of the waves grew loud.

"Stop!" Tenko commanded abruptly.

Out of the greyness ahead loomed a terrifying reef. Quickly Tenko twisted his paddle in the water and turned the craft. The reef stretched northward unbroken, ahead of them. Jagged, toothed rocks revealed themselves. The sweat broke out on Tenko's forehead but no word of fear escaped his lips. By this time he had no idea in which direction they were moving. He could only keep the line of the reefs on his right hand and listen keenly for any change in the sound of the crashing waves. The fog seemed to thicken. The catamaran crept over the sea yard by yard. Tenko could do nothing but hope he would see any outstanding pinnacles of the reef in time.

For a brief moment the mist parted and he could see a few yards ahead. The reef pointed a jagged finger to the north but there seemed to be nothing beyond it. They paddled on. It seemed as if they were reaching open sea.

"Stop!" Tenko called.

They rested their paddles and listened.

"The sea sounds further away on my right. Does it sound like that to you too, Brockan?"

"Yes, Tenko. I think I can hear a dragging sound of shingle and sand too." Brockan's ears were sharp.

"Let us pull towards it," Tenko said, altering the course of the catamaran. "Keep a sharp look-out for rocks."

They dipped their paddles again. The craft moved steadily through the water for about half a mile but still they saw neither reefs nor land. The sound of waves beating on a beach grew louder.

"The water is getting shallower," Tenko declared. He could tell by the drag of his paddle in it.

"The mist is thinning at last!" Kali exclaimed.

They pulled for another few strokes and then Tenko cried, "Steady the craft!"

They thrust out their paddles and steadied it. Tenko pushed his paddle, blade downwards, into the water. "I touched sand!" he cried. "It was soft sand, not hard rock." His voice cracked on a note of relief. "Let us paddle very gently and see if it becomes shallower still."

There was no doubt about it. The shore was shelving

rapidly. Tenko peered over the side of his boat. "There is only enough water to reach just above our knees. I will get out and push the craft. You stay where you are, in case it is only a sandy shoal."

Tenko pushed the boats ahead of him. Another couple of minutes and the catamaran grounded. The waves were curling lazily over a sandy beach.

"Haul up the boats!" Tenko cried.

Kali and Brockan sprang out. Freedom from fear lent strength to their arms. They hauled the catamaran over the wet sand to a slope of dry sand above the tide level. They had reached a bay with another small river running into it. They followed the stream inland for a short distance but there were no signs of either people or herds. They turned back one more to the shore.

"Let us get the meat and drinking horns out of the boats. I am hungry!" Tenko declared.

By the time they had eaten the light began to fail.

"Soon it will be dark," Tenko said. "We shall have to stay here for the night. There is a soft sandy hollow where we can sleep and this bank will give us shelter from the wind."

The children curled up in the hollow and pulled their sheepskin cloaks over them. Soon they were asleep from utter exhaustion.

9. The Day of Fear

Dawn broke early, as it does in the northern islands in summer. Tenko stretched himself and looked about him. The mists were clearing, leaving wisps of cloud over the sea. He could see how lucky they had been the previous day. To the south of them were high forbidding cliffs, to the north an ugly reef of rocks stretching out into the sea. They had struck the one place for miles where they could beach their craft.

He looked at Kali and Brockan, still asleep. Kali stirred, sat up and rubbed her eyes. "Has the fog gone?"

"Yes. It's bright and clear. Let's have a look what lies about us."

Kali shook Brockan by the shoulder.

They climbed up the bank of the stream to a low hill and looked about them. Tenko faced to the north and east. He drew in his breath sharply.

"Round that small island at the end of the reef, the coast bends sharply eastward. Look over there! There is another island! The man from the northern tribes told me the truth."

The long shape of the island stretched itself out as if pointing to the ocean beyond. Great cliffs reared themselves skywards. White sands lay at their feet. Beyond the first island Tenko thought he could discern the shadowy shapes of other islands.

"There must be many islands," Tenko said like one in a dream. "I should like to take the boats and go in search of them."

Kali looked alarmed. "You promised our father that by sunset tonight..." she began.

"I know! I know!" Tenko said heavily. "I will keep my promise, but some day my boats shall ride those northern seas."

Brockan's eyes were searching the land to the south. He exclaimed, "What is that? I can see smoke rising!"

The other two swung round. Sure enough, there was a column of smoke rising from the shores of a gleaming lake, not far from the place where they had slept, but hidden from them by the banks of the stream.

"Smoke can mean only one thing. There are people there. Perhaps they can tell us about the islands to the north." Tenko hesitated. "But will the people be friendly?"

"Lokar says the people of Orkney have not fought with each other for as long as men can remember," Kali reminded him.

"All the same, I think we will hide our boats and not leave them on the open beach," Tenko decided. "There is a small cave in the rocks to the south of the beach were we landed. I can see it from here. Let us pull our boats into it." Some strange instinct advised Tenko to take this precaution. "I think we will not tell the people that we came in boats, either. We will just say we came from the south."

They made their way to the boats. The tide was beginning to fall and they dragged the catamaran through the shallow water to the cave. Tenko looked at the sides of it anxiously. He was glad to find that the high-tide mark only came halfway up the walls. There was a little shelving beach of dry sand at the end of the cave where the boats would be safe. They pulled the craft up on to this and waded back to the shore.

In less than half an hour they reached the place from which the smoke was rising. There were three beehive-shaped houses very like the ones at Skara, half buried in the ground.

Outside one of them sat a group of three men. They were sharpening flint knives. They rose with a shout and came running when they saw the children.

"Who are you? From where have you come?"

Kali answered for them. "We are of the tribe of Skara. We are Birno's children."

One of the men looked at Tenko and gave a start of recognition. "I saw this lad at the Festival of the Sun. He was the lad with the strange axe. I told you about him, Gerth."

"I did not go to the temple of the Sun this year because I have wounded my foot," Gerth explained. "Ingsay here suffers from a sickness of the stomach. That is why Stanga went alone. We are only a small tribe of Saebar."

Gerth seemed to be the head of the tribe. Women and children came out of the huts and gathered round, wide-eyed at the sight of strangers.

"Where did you come from?" Gerth asked.

Tenko pointed vaguely to the south. "From Skara, towards the midday sun."

"It is more than a day's journey, yet you are here before the sun is at its highest. How is that?" Gerth sounded puzzled.

"We slept the night in a hollow by a stream," Tenko replied quite truthfully.

"Why did you come here?" The question was sharp this time.

"We wanted to see what country lay to the north of Skara. There was a man at the Festival of the Sun to whom I talked. He came from a northern tribe. He told me many islands lay to the north. I wanted to see for myself," Tenko replied.

"There was a man from the tribe of Bowana at the Festival. I saw him talking to this lad," Stanga affirmed. "The tribe of Bowana live north of the rising sun. I have heard him tell, too, of many islands beyond his coast."

"You will be hungry after your journey. Have you eaten?" Gerth asked. It was the custom in Orkney to offer food to men from another tribe.

The children realised they were indeed hungry. Beyond a drink from the stream they had had no breakfast. They had been too eager to discover the source of the smoke.

"Yes, we are hungry," Kali said.

"Then you will eat with us," Gerth invited them.

The women brought out milk in bowls and meat from the huts. The children drank thirstily and ate the meat. The tribe stood round watching them. Gerth took a drink of milk and gnawed at a bone also. This was the ceremony of hospitality. When he had shown that friendship was extended he asked Tenko a question.

"What have you done with your strange axe? Stanga told me of it. Have you got it with you?"

Rather unwillingly Tenko drew the axe from the large pocket inside his tunic.

"I should like to look at it," Gerth said, putting out his hand.

Tenko could hardly refuse, since they had eaten together. Reluctantly he handed it over. Gerth turned it about and cautiously ran his thumb along its keen edge. He was astonished to find it so sharp.

"What kind of stone is this?" he asked Tenko.

"It is not stone at all."

"How is it made then?"

"I do not know. I have never seen one made. My father got it from a man of a tribe to the south. He told my father it was made by melting some strange kind of stone in a fierce fire."

Gerth looked incredulous. "I cannot believe it. Stone will not melt in a fire."

"That is what I was told," Tenko answered stubbornly. "The

man from Bowana told me there were islands far, far away to the north where men had bronze axes like mine. That is why I am seeking the islands. I want to learn the secret of how my axe was made. Other things might perhaps be made in the same way, knives and pins."

"I journeyed part of the way home with the man from Bowana," Stanga said. "As we walked, we talked of the axe this lad carried. The man told me he had been in a skin boat to Rousa, the island of hills you can see from the north coast. There he found people who were clever at making things with their hands. They made cups of a different shape from ours."

Tenko felt at last that he was on the track of discovery.

"What tribe were these people?" he asked.

"He said they were of the tribe of Rinyo. They dwell under the shadow of a great headland to the north."

"Did the men of Rinyo make bronze axes such as this?" Tenko asked.

"No. But the man told me the folk of Rinyo said there were many more islands to the north, beyond our sight. Men had come across the great eastern sea to them in strange boats, much bigger than our skin boats."

The children exchanged quick glances but they did not mention their craft hidden in the cave. Something warned them to be silent.

Tenko could not keep the excitement out of his voice. "Tell me more about these people."

"I cannot tell you much; only what the man of Bowana told me. The men of Rinyo had told him that the men from across the eastern sea carried shining axes and bright knives, not made of stone like ours," Stanga said.

"I must go to the island of Rousa," Tenko said with determination.

"How would you get there, my lad?" Gerth's voice was sharp.

Tenko almost bit his tongue to keep the words from tumbling out about his two log-boats. "I could make a skin boat out of the bones of oxen and their hides," he said lamely.

"That is a good thought," Gerth said. "If you learn how your axe is made, will you come back this way and show us how it is done?"

"Yes, I might do that," Tenko said a little boastfully.

"Then you will lend us your axe till you come back?" Gerth asked craftily. "It is usual to make a gift when you have eaten with a friendly tribe."

Tenko saw the trap into which he had fallen. "Oh, I could never give away my axe," he said quickly. He stretched out his hand for the axe again but Gerth held on to it.

"I am not asking you to give it," he said. "I only ask you to lend it till you can make me another."

He held the axe menacingly, its edge towards Tenko. Kali put her hand to her mouth in alarm. Brockan bit his lip. Tenko decided it would be dangerous to try to snatch back the axe. He must match cunning with cunning.

"Very well," he agreed. "Will you give me a hide and bones in exchange, to make a skin boat?"

"Yes. You shall have that, but you will have to wait till I kill an ox."

"We will wait. May we sleep at your hut?"

"Yes, you shall sleep on the floor of my hut," Gerth agreed.

"But, Tenko, we promised my father..." Kali was beginning, but Tenko silenced her with a gesture and a frown.

As the sun began to sink, Gerth led them to his hut. Tenko walked beside Kali.

"What shall we do, Tenko?" Kali whispered.

"Listen, Kali! Wait till everyone is asleep. Then you and

Brockan must creep out of the hut silently. Make your way to the cave where the boats are hidden. If the tide is high, you may have to wait to get to them."

"But what will you do, Tenko?" Kali muttered back.

"I will try to get my axe. Hide behind the rocks on the shore and wait for me. If I have not come by the time the sun is risen you must get the boats out and try to make your way back to Skara."

"Without you?" Kali sounded desperate.

"Yes, without me! You are to do as I bid you, Kali. I must do my best to get you back to Skara as I promised our father."

Kali gulped back the tears. "I will tell Brockan when I get a chance."

That night they were lodged in Gerth's own hut. Tenko was relieved to find there was only a short passage leading to it. The huts were poor compared with those of Skara. There were no stone dressers nor beds. There was a fire in the centre and Gerth's family slept round it on heather beds covered by sheepskins. Tenko was glad of this. It might make escape easier. He remembered with satisfaction that Gerth was limping from a sore foot.

Heather beds were made for the strangers and the children lay down. Kali was beside Brockan but Tenko was on the other side of the hearth beside Gerth. Gerth put the bronze axe under his pile of heather and lay upon it. Everyone settled down to sleep. Though Kali and Brockan pretended to sleep too, they were alert and waking. For two hours, Tenko bided his time. Then cautiously he raised himself on his elbow and peered round him by the light of the smouldering fire. Kali lifted her head too and laid a warning hand on Brockan. Nobody else stirred. All round them the sleepers breathed evenly. Gerth was snoring. Tenko sat up and pointed to the passage. Kali saw him through the trembling air and smoke above the fire. Lithe as a fox she slipped to her feet and pulled at Brockan's arm. He was up in one single noiseless movement. They waited a minute to see if anyone else stirred, but no one did. On tiptoe, picking their way round the recumbent bodies by the firelight, they reached the low narrow passage. Kali stooped and led the way. She and Brockan disappeared like mice down a hole. When he was sure they were clear Tenko breathed a sigh of relief. He must give them time to reach the beach before he made the next move.

Tenko waited for a full hour. He knew by then that in the northern summer it would be dawn. His plan was to create confusion and fear in the hut and to make Gerth rise from his bed. A bone shovel lay near the smouldering fire. Suddenly Tenko leaped to his feet and snatched the shovel. With it he lifted a smouldering peat and placed it at the foot of Gerth's heather bed. The heather was dry. In a minute it caught fire and began to crackle. This was the moment for Tenko. He shook Gerth by the shoulder.

"Gerth! Get up! Get up! Your bed has caught fire!"

Gerth woke with a jerk, heard the crackling and saw the flames. He sprang to his feet. Tenko was already trying to beat out the fire with the shovel and shouting as he did so. The other occupants of the hut woke. Smoke was filling the hut. There was instant confusion. The older people rushed to beat out the flames too. The children rushed for the passage and fell tumbling out of the hut. Tenko still smacked at the burning heather bed with his shovel. He felt the shovel hit something hard. He knew in a flash that it was his axe and he snatched it from the smouldering heather. Like a hare he fled across the hut and down the narrow passage. The smoke hid his flight from Gerth, who was still beating out the flames.

He had just got the fire out when the children came back shouting into the hut.

"The stranger! The stranger boy!" they yelled. "He ran out carrying the shining axe!"

Gerth swooped on what was left of his bed and kicked the heather aside. The axe was gone. He ran out from the hut shouting, "Which way did the lad go? Which way?"

A boy pointed towards the shore. "He went leaping and running down there."

"The other two children? Were they with him?"

The boy shook his head. "I did not see them."

Gerth shook his fist. "They will not get far on the beach. The rocks will cut them off to the north and to the south. We shall soon find them." He snatched up a whip of hide that was beside the door. "When I catch Tenko I shall round him up like an ox," he declared cruelly. He began to run down the hill, but his sore foot impeded him. The rest of the tribe streamed after him, not daring to overtake him in his wrath.

Tenko had counted on his start and on his quicker turn of speed. He made for the stream and ran along the bank above it. He knew it would bring him out at the sandy beach. Though he did not pause, he watched his footing carefully. If he stumbled and fell the pack might catch up with him. He could hear their yells behind him. At last the stream spread itself on the shore. Tenko scrambled down to the beach.

"Where are you, Kali? Brockan!" he cried.

Tenko knew they would make for the rocks near the cave. He ran faster, leaping over the rock pools.

"Kali! Brockan!" he cried again.

They appeared suddenly from behind a rock.

"Run! Run for the cave! We must get the boats out before Gerth reaches the beach!"

"Look, Tenko!" Brockan cried.

Tenko had forgotten that the tide would be higher than it had been a dawn the previous day. The water lapped round the mouth of the cave! It would be too deep for Brockan to wade through it.

"Wade out to the cave as far as you can go!" Tenko shouted. "I will go and bring the boats."

He thrust his axe into Kali's hands and splashed his way through the channels, the children following him. Soon he was up to his waist and began to swim vigorously. He reached the mouth of the cave and disappeared inside.

Fear lent him strength. He hauled the catamaran down the steeply shelving bank to the lapping water. Seizing a paddle he thrust it into deeper water and then pulled himself aboard. A few rapid strokes brought it to the mouth of the cave. He glanced across the sandy bay. The tribe of Saebar was streaming down from the sand dunes. In two or three minutes they would catch up with the wading children.

"Swim to me! Swim to me!" he shouted to Kali and Brockan. "Drop the axe, Kali, and swim to me!"

For once Kali disobeyed Tenko. She gripped the handle of the axe between her teeth and swam for dear life with Brockan after her. Tenko hauled them aboard as Gerth began to wade out after them.

"Your axe, Tenko!" Kali held it out to him.

Tenko flung it into the bottom of his boat. "Take your paddles and paddle your hardest!" he yelled.

Tenko brought the catamaran round with a sweep of his paddle and they headed for the open sea.

The tribe of Saebar stopped dead, almost as one man, astonished at the sight of the strange craft. Gerth recovered himself and shouted for them to go after the strangers. He began to swim powerfully, but the distance between him and the catamaran widened. He stopped swimming and stood shoulder-deep in the water threatening them with his fist.

"I am sorry I had to set fire to your bed, Gerth," Tenko yelled back. "I had to have my axe back. When I have learned the secret of how the axe was made I will make you another." Tenko was quite sincere, but Gerth gnashed his teeth in rage.

As Kali bent her paddle her heart was singing for joy. She was remembering that Tenko had told her to drop the axe rather than impede her own escape. In that instant she knew that though the axe was dear to Tenko's heart, she was dearer still.

The sun was setting when they reached the Bay of Skaill. It was with joy that they saw the tops of the huts of Skara once more. As they came into the bay they were sighted by Birno, who had Stempsi beside him. They had watched all night and all day with despair at their hearts. Birno knew something must have happened, for he knew Tenko would not otherwise break his promise to him to return on the second day. There had been mist over the sea. In that case Birno knew Tenko would try to put ashore, but Birno knew what a cruel shore it was and his heart misgave him. All the same he had great faith in Tenko and he did not give up hope.

Birno gave a mighty shout when he saw the catamaran coming in across the bay, the three children outlined against the setting sun. He waded into the water to meet them. Stempsi with him. Birno's shout had brought the rest of the tribe running. Arms were outstretched in welcome. Willing hands hauled the boats ashore and the three adventurers were borne in gladness to the village.

That night there was a great feast of rejoicing over their safe return. When the other folk had departed to their own huts

Tenko talked with Lokar and Birno. When Tenko told how Gerth had taken the axe from him and held them prisoners, Birno's face darkened into an ugly scowl.

"The men of Skara will go overland to the tribe of Saebar. I will see that Gerth gets a fitting punishment," he declared.

Lokar laid a hand on Birno's arm. "No, my son! That could begin fighting between tribes that might go on for many generations. You would bring war to Orkney. That you must never do. Birno, I have always taught you the ways of peace. My end is not far off now. Do not let me leave life in sorrow."

Birno calmed down. "Very well, Lokar. I will heed your words."

"What did you learn from your journey, Tenko?" Lokar asked.

"I learned many things from Stanga of the tribe of Saebar: that there are many islands to the north. I saw some of these myself from a high cliff. I learned, too, that there are islands far, far beyond these, to the north. To these islands people have come from lands across the great sea to the east. These people know how to make axes of bronze like mine, so Stanga had heard."

"These are wise things to know, Tenko. It was good that you went on this voyage. What you have learned will be of great use to you in days to come. Out of it will come good for those who remain of the tribe of Skara. And now you must sleep, for you are weary indeed."

Kali and Brockan were already asleep. Tenko lay down on the bed he shared with Brockan and soon he was fast asleep too.

10. The Night of Doom

It was in the autumn of the year that Tenko had made his voyage in search of the northern islands. The people of Skara were making ready for the winter. They cut peats from the black bog-lands and carried them to the settlement. There they were neatly stacked round the outer walls to strengthen them.

The herdsmen slaughtered cattle and sheep and the women salted down the meat. In bitter weather snow and frost covered the grazing lands so the Skara folk always killed off part of their herds. Fresh heather had been cut in late summer and the beds had been renewed. Out of the skins of the slaughtered animals the women were making winter garments. This time they did not scrape off the wool but left it on for additional warmth. Now it was late October and the days were shorter and the nights long.

There were sad gatherings round the fire on these nights for there were no more tales from Lokar. Lokar was dying. He had lived longer than any man remembered. Now his old heart had grown feeble and his limbs would no longer carry him.

One night when Birno was watching beside him Lokar stirred restlessly and said, "Bring Tenko!"

"It is night and Tenko is fast asleep," Birno told him gently.

"My time is getting short, Birno. Bring Tenko! I have things I must say to you both."

Birno woke Tenko. "Come quietly. Do not wake the rest. Lokar wants you."

They went silently as ghosts to Lokar's hut.

"Sit beside me," Lokar said. He took a hand of each as though he drew strength from them. "Now I am near death I can see and understand things better than ever before. What is to come is shown to me in part. I must tell it to you."

Birno and Tenko bent lower so they did not miss a whisper.

"Death and destruction are coming to Skara. You must watch for the signs for I shall no longer be with you. You will know them when they appear. There will be a great wind. Skara will vanish in a night but it will not be lost for ever. The same power which overwhelms it will restore it, but not for many, many winters and summers."

"You are very ill, Lokar. It is your illness that makes you imagine terrible things," Birno told him.

"It is my illness that gives me the sight. Take heart, though, Birno. Not all of you will perish. When the night of doom comes, listen to Tenko. Do not scorn him because he is young. He will know what to do." Lokar looked towards Tenko. "Tenko, you will do your utmost for my people?"

"I promise you, Lokar."

"In you and Kali and Brockan will rest the future of the tribe of Skara. Be a son always to Birno and Stempsi." He turned once more to Birno. "Birno, will you take me to the Place of the Dead at Maeshowe?"

"Yes, Lokar. Your bones shall rest with the chiefs and wise men of Orkney."

"I am content."

Not long afterwards Lokar sank into a deep sleep from which he did not wake. There was great sorrow among the people of Skara. There was sorrow indeed among all the tribes of Orkney when word was sent to them. Lokar had been the wisest High Priest of the Sun that Orkney had ever known.

It was a sad procession that set off from Skara to trudge

the miles to Maeshowe. Birno and the strong men of the tribe carried Lokar's body on a stretcher made of sheepskin. Behind them came the rest of the men and boys. The stone symbols of the Sun were carried cupped in the palms of the men, but Tenko carried his bronze axe, polished so that it shone in the wintry sun. So they came to the Place of the Dead, the great mound of Maeshowe. There they were met by men of other tribes, come to do honour to Lokar.

It was the first time Tenko had been to Maeshowe. He had seen it at a distance when the Festival of the Sun took place. The great green mound was shaped like a cone and rose high above the surrounding plain. Round the mound was a broad ditch, forty-five feet wide and six feet deep. There was a road across it to a doorway closed by a stone slab.

The stretcher bearers laid down their burden outside the door and removed the stone slab. It revealed a long narrow stone tunnel. A man from a nearby settlement came carrying a bowl of smouldering peats. Four young men carried torches of sheep's wool dipped in whale oil and bound to long bones. The young men kindled them at the bowl of peats; then, stooping, they went first to light the way into the great tomb. Only two men could carry the stretcher now, for the passage was only three feet wide. Birno took the foremost ends of the bone supports and Lemba brought up the rear. They carried Lokar to his last resting place. As they disappeared into the tunnel the tribes set up a sad wailing and keening that rose and fell like the wind.

Tenko followed the men down the tunnel. To his astonishment they arrived in a great square chamber. The burning torches revealed lofty walls of great stone slabs placed one above the other, with edges projecting to make a beehive roof. Tenko caught his breath at the size of the

143

place and the immensity of the slabs of stone that built it. There were three large openings in the walls, two of them closed by slabs of stone. The entrance to the third was open and a massive wedge-shaped block of stone lay below it. Into this cell Birno lifted Lokar's body and placed him in his last resting place. As he did so a terrible sad cry broke from the lips of the men of Orkney. It was their last salutation to Lokar. The cry was repeated three times. Tenko trembled. It was a cry that sent a cold shiver down his spine.

Once more the tomb was closed by the stone and Birno sealed the gaps with wet clay. A great shivering sigh broke from all the men in the Place of the Dead as the flames of the torches began to die. Then the men turned and in silence stumbled their way out of the darkness of the tunnel into the sunshine.

It was a quiet company that made its way back to Skara. Birno felt glad when at last Tenko broke the silence with a question.

"Who built the great Place of the Dead at Maeshowe?"

"Men of our tribes long, long ago. Lokar told us once that they came from the shores of a great sea to the south. There, it is said, are other tombs of the pattern of Maeshowe."

"Those great blocks of stone must have been difficult to quarry and to set in position," Tenko remarked.

"That is true. The men of those days had great skills in handling stones and in building, greater perhaps than we have now."

"Some of their skill and knowledge must have come to you. Remember, you shaped and raised some of the great stones of Brodgar," Tenko reminded him.

Birno smiled a little. "Who knows from where we draw our knowledge and our skill? Father teaches son and the son teaches his son and so it goes on through many, many lives. Now and again some man discovers some new things and adds it to what men know already."

"I wonder if the people who built Maeshowe knew how to make bronze axes too?" Tenko said.

"I do not think so," Birno said. "If they did, surely some careless worker would have left his bronze axe lying about and we should have found it." He laughed a little. "You are still troubling who made your bronze axe, Tenko?"

"Some day I shall find the men who can make axes like this one. I will not rest till I do," Tenko told him.

Birno shook his head. "I do not think you will find them in Orkney."

As they reached Skara the sun was setting. There were hump-shaped clouds on the horizon and the sea heaved and moaned with a heavy ground swell. There was an uncanny stillness in the air and a shimmering over the sea. Birno looked over the great expanse of water.

"It is a strange sky and sea tonight," he remarked, giving a shiver. "Perhaps winter is coming on us already."

As if to affirm his words a chill wind blew out of the west making cat's paws on the water. It was the beginning.

The people of Skara did not linger in the meeting place as they might have done at other times. Perhaps they were weighed down with the burden of mourning for Lokar: perhaps the chill of winter was already entering a little into their bones, but they went quietly to their own huts.

Stempsi blew on the peats and grilled steaks of mutton at the end of a long bone that served as a toasting fork, while Kali warmed milk in a bowl. They ate in silence. Suddenly Birno raised his head. "The wind is rising," he said.

They listened. The sound had grown to a steady whine.

The thatch of rushes and turf that Birno had laid over the jaws of whalebone rustled and rattled as if a rat were among them. The pitch of the wind's whine grew higher.

"It sounds like a storm blowing up," Stempsi remarked.

Tenko rose to his feet. "I will go down to the beach and see that the boats are well pulled up."

"I will come too and help you," Birno said.

When they reached the sand dunes the wind whistled about their ears. The bent marram grasses quivered and rustled: the sea heaved and twisted, flecked with spume. It seemed as if the whole world was stirring, uneasy and menacing.

They went down to the beach. The waves were breaking hard on the distant reefs and there was a heavy drag of shingle in the undertow on the beach. It was still low tide. Some instinct told Tenko to lift the boats to some other place instead of just above the high-water mark on the beach.

"Let us carry them to the rocks that are close in to the shore at the place where the stream of Skara flows into the sea," Tenko suggested. "The tide never covers those rocks."

"Yes, we will do that," Birno agreed.

It meant carrying the boats nearly a quarter of a mile to the south of the Bay of Skaill. Tenko and Birno bent their backs to the task. It was a grim struggle. The wind was blowing off the sea against them, a cold biting wind that raised little scurries of sand and blew it into their eyes. Their lips were gritty and salt with the feel and taste of it. At last, breathless, they reached the rock well above high-water mark. There, in the shelter of the rock they had a brief respite from the wind.

"Here there is a curved bite out of the rock facing the land. Let us put the boat here," Tenko suggested.

They stowed the boat under the lee of the rock.

"Lift one or two big boulders, Birno, and put them inside the craft."

"Why? Do you think the wind will blow it away?" Birno laughed. "It would take a mighty storm indeed to lift a boat like that."

"There is no telling how far tonight's tide might reach," Tenko said seriously.

Suddenly Birno remembered Lokar's words and felt uneasy. He helped Tenko to fill his boat with ballast.

They made a second journey with the smaller boat. By the time they returned to the huts of Skara the moon had risen and was casting a fitful light over the turmoil of sea. Their faces were stung by the scouring sand as Birno and Tenko fought their way back to the huts. There was a thin drifting of sand along the tunnel.

"Kali and Stempsi will have plenty to do sweeping the sand away tomorrow," Birno remarked.

Tenko said nothing but he cast an anxious glance backwards over the sand dunes.

Already Stempsi, Kali and Brockan had gone to their stone bunks. Strange gusty noises came from the thatch. Tenko crept in beside Brockan but he could not sleep. The peat fire glowed a little more brightly than usual, as though the draughts along the tunnel would not let it sleep either. Tenko lifted himself up on an elbow, watching the fire and thinking of many things. The wind rose again. It seemed to Tenko as though wordless voices wailed to them from out of the sea. A shrill note rose above all the others, an undulating warning note. It seemed to summon up a sudden surge of sound. There was a roar of wind and sea in wild thunder. Suddenly it ceased and sank to a murmur, fading almost to silence. Then, once again, there was a low stirring of sound, growing and growing till it howled and shrieked in a turmoil. From the sea came a dull boom with an eerie echo among the reefs. Under the stone slab door to the tunnel was a gap. Through it drifted a sifting of sand. It twisted in tiny whirlwinds just inside the hut. The wind died to a sudden silence again. Tenko began to think the storm was dying away. Then, all at once, the wind rose in a mocking shriek. The sea answered, crashing in fury. The skirl of the wind mounted higher and higher. Like a blow from a mighty hammer the wind hit the beehive roof of the hut and lifted part of the thatch and whirled it away.

Everyone was wakened by the noise. Birno sprang from his bed. "What was that?"

"The wind has taken some of the thatch," said Tenko.

Birno surveyed the damage. "There is a big hole, but the whalebone frame seems firm. We shall have repairs to do tomorrow."

Once again the wind died down, only to rise to a sudden onslaught of fury. A small cloud of sand blew in through the hole and fell upon the fire.

"It is the worst wind we have ever known," Stempsi said anxiously.

The wind came funnelling through the hole, bringing another choking cloud of sand and scattering some of the smouldering peats. Tenko and Birno ran hither and thither stamping them out. They could hardly see each other through the drifting rain of sand.

The whole stone hut seemed to quiver as the wind dealt it buffeting blows. The wailing note of the storm rose higher and higher as though all the demons of the air had been let loose. There came another ominous crack from the roof.

"Quick! On to your beds under the shelter of the walls!" Birno cried.

They cowered under the beehive-like slabs of stone. The wind battered the remaining thatch, lifting it up and down. Then there came a terrible crash. Down into the hut fell the great jaws of whalebone, bringing with them showers of sand. For a minute the peats blazed up as the remaining thatch caught fire, adding smoke to the whirlwind of sand. The family choked and spluttered, hiding their faces under their arms.

The hut was now wide open to the storm. Even inside the wind shivered and howled, bringing with it so much sand that it dowsed the fire.

"We cannot stay here," Stempsi said. "I can hardly breathe."

"I will go and see if the folks in the other huts have fared any better," Tenko said, snatching up his cloak from the bed.

He found drifts of sand along the tunnel passage, into which his feet sank. When he reached the end there was a drift that came halfway up the entrance. He squirmed his way through to the main passage. Even here he could not stand upright for the drifted sand. In the meeting place a small crowd of people had gathered, confused, frightened.

"How is it with you?" Tenko asked. "Our roof has been carried away."

"All the thatches have gone," Lemba told him. "The houses are filling with sand. What are we to do, Tenko?"

"I will go back and bring Birno," Tenko said.

There was a slight lull in the wind, so instead of going straight back, he made his way along the passage that led to the sand dunes. Tenko felt he had to see what was happening outside. He covered his nostrils with his sheepskin cloak and stepped from under cover. Even though the wind had dropped a little the sand stung him pitilessly. It seemed as if the whole world was in motion. The sand dunes were heaving up and down like giant waves, piling up sand against the stone huts. Some drifts were level with the holes on the roofs and the sand was pouring down into the huts below in a constant stream. A whole sandbank was threatening Birno's house. Tenko saw what was bound to happen. There was no time to lose. He fought his way back along the passage. When he reached the tunnel to Birno's hut he almost passed it by. A drift was within inches of the top of the entrance. Tenko scooped aside the sand with his hands as fast as he could and worked his way on his hands and knees to the hut.

"Quick! Quick! Get out of here!" he cried. "The sand dunes are shifting and burying the huts! They are all on the move like the sea. You'll be buried alive if you stay!"

Even as Birno and the others sprang to their feet a stream of sand poured through the hole where the thatch had been. It almost smothered them as it fell, spreading over the floor of the hut.

Birno seized Stempsi. "Hold on to my tunic, Brockan!" he shouted above the crash and thunder of the tempest above. "Bring Kali, Tenko!"

They dashed for the opening to the tunnel, climbing over a mound of sand. Tenko followed, pulling Kali by the hand. When they reached the door Kali gave a shriek. Something had seized her by the throat and was pulling her back from Tenko.

"Come on! Come on!" Tenko cried, tugging at her.

"I can't! My beads have caught in the stone. They're choking me."

Tenko turned round, made a grab in the darkness and

caught hold of the string of bone beads. He wrenched them apart and they went cascading to the ground. Kali was freed.

"Oh, my necklace! You gave it to me!" Kali cried, stopping to scoop up her beads. Tenko jerked her roughly to her feet.

"Come on, Kali! There is no time! Quick, along the passage before it is filled with sand! If you stop for your beads, you will be buried alive with them." He pushed her along before him. They had barely gone a few paces when there was a roar and the banked-up sand crashed down into the hut. Gasping and spluttering, spitting out sand, the family crawled on hands and knees through the main passage and along to the meeting place. This was open to the sky and was already knee-deep in sand. The folk were there trying to fight their way back to the huts to get some shelter.

"Out! Out!" Birno cried. "Get out of your houses or the sand will bury you!" He drove them before him like a flock of sheep. They struggled out on to the shifting, billowing sand dunes.

"Oh, where shall we go? What shall we do?" Stempsi cried. In the darkness and sandstorm all was confusion.

"Keep hold of each other's arms," Birno cried. "Do not let go! We will pull each other up if we stumble."

Lemba hooked his arm on to Brockan's. It was difficult to know where they were in all that turmoil of land and sea. Tenko thought quickly.

"I know a place where we might be safe," he cried. "Keep heading into the wind. Do not turn your backs on it. Above all hold on to each other." Tenko knew that so long as they kept their faces to the wind, they would be heading westward and sooner or later they would encounter some landmark.

"No! No!" Tresko cried. "We must turn our backs on the

wind and run before it. That stupid lad knows nothing! He will lead you to your death in the sea. Every man for himself and run!"

Most of the tribe of Skara obeyed him, for it was easier to turn their backs than to face the stinging, lashing sand. The minute they left the slight shelter the huts afforded, the wind took those who were not holding on to each other and who had turned their backs to it. It bowled them over, lifting them bodily off their feet. It rolled them over and over like balls. Singly there was no standing against it. Like spindrift they were borne before it. The old and the children soon fell and were unable to rise. The sand fell thickly upon them. Soon they were suffocated by it. They lay, strange mounds and shrouded forms on the ground. The sand blew over them and covered them like snow.

Clinging desperately to each other, Birno's family and Lemba fought their way into the teeth of the storm, bending towards the wind. Their feet sank deep into sand drifts. It was like struggling through a bog. At last they reached a rocky hollow in the lee of a small hill.

"Let us stop to get our breath," Birno said.

Breathing hard, they struggled to clear their mouths and eyes of sand.

"Shall we stay here?" Lemba suggested. "We could lie down here."

"No!" Tenko pointed at the layer of sand which had already drifted into the hollow. "A shift of the wind and we should all be covered as we lay there. No, we must push on!"

Birno remembered what Lokar had said about trusting and obeying Tenko when the doom fell upon Skara.

"We will do as Tenko says. We will push on," he said.

There came another lull in the tempest.

"Let us go now while the wind has dropped," Tenko urged.

They plodded on, linked together by their arms, Birno and Lemba at each end of the line, Tenko thrusting forward in the middle like the point of an arrow, with Kali, Stempsi and Brockan on each side. All at once their feet began to move on a slope downhill, the wind seemed to whistle more overhead and the sting of the sand was not so cutting.

"Feel carefully with your feet now," Tenko advised them.

Hardly were the words out of his mouth than he slipped himself, dragging the others after him. From below came the sound of running water. They slipped feet first down a steeply sloping bank and fell into shallow muddy water at its foot.

"Oh, where are we now?" Stempsi cried in terror.

Tenko let out a shout of joy. "We've found it! We've found it! Do not fear, Stempsi! This is the place I sought."

"Where are we?" Kali asked.

"This is the stream of Skara."

"But the sand is blowing up the stream, filling the space between the banks like a snowdrift," Birno said doubtfully. "If we stay here, it could bury us."

"We will not stay. Keep hold of each other and wade up the stream," Tenko said. "It is shallow but there are one or two pools into which you might fall."

They made a human chain with Tenko leading them. Mercifully the wind eased a little. Tenko felt his way among the boulders of the stream, putting down a cautious foot whenever he thought a pool might lie before them. Sometimes they were up to their waists in water; sometimes the stream barely covered their ankles. The worst danger was the drifted sand which had sunk to the bottom of the stream and clogged their feet. The wind began to rise again. The banks of the stream had grown shallower and once more the stinging sand beat upon them.

"Perhaps we could find more shelter lower down the stream..." Birno was beginning, when the moon appeared for a minute from behind thick cloud and light filtered through the sandstorm. Tenko gave a cry of relief.

"There it is! The rock where the stream bends."

A large rock loomed up in their way. The wind almost blew them into it. Tenko pressed on round it. Suddenly the wind seemed to have left them. The stream had taken a complete right-angled bend round the rock.

"This is the place I wanted to find," Tenko gasped.

The stream came tumbling down from the Hill of Yettna above, cutting deep banks. These banks lay at opposite points of the compass from the direction of the wind. The wind went howling past the bend of the stream leaving them in an oasis of comparative calm where the rock jutted out.

The bank behind it curved round a rocky pool.

"Keep close to the rock," Tenko warned them. "The pool below is deep."

They found a flat stone where they could all sit in the lee of the great rock, sheltered from the storm and the driving sand. For a few minutes they did not speak from sheer exhaustion. Then Birno asked, "How did you know of this place, Tenko?"

"I came to try to get a fish in this deep pool last summer. While I was here a rainstorm blew up out of the west. The rock sheltered me till it was over. I remembered it when we fled from Skara. I thought it might give us shelter now."

They sat huddled together, waiting for the dawn to break.

11. The Day of Decision

When daylight came at last it filtered through a veil of flying sand. It was as if fog hid the landscape from them. The wind had lessened but it still blew hard.

"We must wait for the wind to drop before we leave the shelter of the rock," Birno decided.

They crept down to the pool and drank. The water tasted brackish but at least it slaked their thirst. They huddled together for warmth and waited for the storm to subside. All that day the wind blew and they peeped out from behind the rock at the sandstorms scudding across the opposite low hill. They said little, but hunger grew in them. It seemed a long time since they had eaten supper in the hut. At last night fell. Kali and Stempsi huddled together inside Stempsi's sheepskin cape, which she had snatched up when they fled. The men and boys kept close for warmth. They slept fitfully, uneasily. Birno lay awake, wondering what had happened to his home.

At last dawn streaked a pale grey sky with primrose. Tenko rubbed his eyes and sat up. The wind had dropped to a slight breeze. He shook Birno.

"Birno, the storm is over."

Birno woke and rubbed his stomach. "I am so hungry I could eat an ox whole!" Then he remembered. "The cattle, Tenko! When the storm broke Salik had herded them all into the enclosures. Let us get back to Skara at once and see what is left to us."

They all crossed the stream below the pool and made their way over the hillside to Skara. The grass of the hill was covered by sand. When they topped the hillock and looked towards Skara they gasped and cried out aloud.

"Skara has vanished!" Stempsi exclaimed.

"Where is our hut? Where is our hut?" Brockan cried, near to tears.

Already Birno and Lemba were running down the hillside. They ploughed through drifts of sand which reached above their knees. When they reached the place where the village had been it was as though a whole sandbank had been rolled over it. Below, where the pebbly beach had once been, the sea reached higher than it had ever done before. A great wall of sand was piled up where the sloping green land had once been. Not a thing stirred about the place that had been Skara.

"It is all gone!" Birno exclaimed.

"All gone!" Lemba echoed. "All the pots I made and the oven where I baked them!"

"We will go to look for the sheep and oxen," Birno said.

They trudged through the sand, slipping and stumbling, towards the pasture. Suddenly Kali pointed a finger.

"Look! Is that the top of the wall of the enclosure?"

They ran to it and scraped away at the sand. It was the enclosure. With their bare hands and a stone prised from the tope of the wall they dug away the sand from a mound inside the enclosure. The horns of a cow emerged. When they got the head free the poor beast's mouth and nose were choked with sand. She must have collapsed on her knees and died where they found her. Kali recognised their favourite black milk cow. "She's dead! She's dead!" she cried and wept bitterly.

"They will all be dead," Birno said stonily. "All our cattle and sheep are gone! Not one left!"

"Let us push on towards the Loch of Skaill and see if we can find any of our people," Lemba suggested.

They made their way over the rising ground, now like a mass of sand dunes. They came on several shapeless lumps buried in the sand. Birno scraped away the covering of sand from one. Stempsi let out a cry.

"It is Ilona! How many times have we laughed and sung together as we worked on our sheepskins! If only she had come with us!" Stempsi buried her face in her hands.

There were many other pitiful buried mounds in the sand. At last they came to one body only partly covered. Birno turned it over. It was Tresko. Like all the others and like the cattle and sheep he had been suffocated by the blowing sand and had fallen as he tried to make his way through it.

"There is nothing we can do. Our people are gone!" Birno said heavily.

Brockan began to weep aloud. "I ... I am so hungry," he sobbed like the small boy he was.

This brought Birno back to their own immediate needs. "Have we lived through the storm only to die of hunger?" he said bitterly.

"We can still find limpets on the rocks," Tenko reminded him.

"If there are any rocks left uncovered by the sand!" Birno shook his head.

"Perhaps we could eat the dead cattle we found under the sand?" Tenko suggested.

Birno shook his head. "It is against the laws of our tribe to eat meat that has died."

"Let us go back again to the stream of Skara," Tenko said. "We can make our way along its bank to the shore. The sand is not so deep there."

They plodded back. It was heavy going till they reached the

stream. Even then they had to wade through mud and wet sand till they reached the place where the stream widened out and ran into the sea. The tide was low. They edged their way round the rocky point of Yettna and found one or two rocks from which they managed to prise enough limpets to take the edge off their hunger.

"We cannot live on limpets alone," Birno said.

Tenko had been looking about him. He gave a cry of joy. "There is the rock where we hid the boats, Birno! The point of it is well up out of the sand. If we could dig down below it..."

He, Lemba and Birno hurried as fast as they could over the sand drifts, plunging to their knees. When they reached the rock they found a hollow scooped in the sand at the base of it. The rock had made a kind of barrier against the worst of the drifts. Behind it the boats were certainly covered by sand but they could not be very far below. They all set to work, scraping sand into their cloaks, lifting it and flinging it clear. Suddenly Kali's hand touched something hard. She gave a cry of joy.

"The boat! I touched the boat then!"

They redoubled their efforts. It was indeed the small boat they were uncovering. Scooping madly with their hands they got it free of the sand at last. They turned it over to empty the sand out of the inside. As they did so Brockan gave an exclamation of delight and pounced on objects that came tumbling out.

"My bow and arrows!" he cried, jumping for joy. "I forgot I had left them there. Now at least we can catch flatfish!"

"We can catch something bigger than flatfish," Tenko declared. "If you will let me have the bow, Brockan, I will go hunting. First, though, let us try to free the bigger boat."

It took much hard work and it was some hours before they finally dug the boat out.

"Here are the paddles undamaged," Tenko said thankfully. He stood for a moment, lost in thought. "Once when I was looking for trout along the stream of Skara a deer came down to the stream to drink. That high hill slopes downward to the east. It may have escaped the worst of the storms out of the west. Perhaps there may still be deer there. I will go to see."

"I will come with you," Birno said. "The rest of you stay here by the boats. See if you can find more limpets and perhaps a crab."

He and Tenko made their way along by the stream of Skara and past the place by the great rock where they had sheltered. The stream grew narrower and the sides steeper. Tenko drew Birno into the shelter of a rock.

"Here is the place I saw the deer. Let us keep very still and see if he comes down to drink again. The wind will blow our scent away from him here."

All Tenko's old instincts of a hunter came back to him.

They waited for an hour, scarcely moving at all. Then Tenko laid a quiet hand on Birno's arm. He pointed along the hill on the other side of the stream. Among the brown bracken and tawny tufts of grass something was stirring. A young deer came bounding down the hillside to the stream. Tenko stiffened, his bow extended. The moment the deer lowered his head to drink, Tenko let fly his arrow. It penetrated the animal's throat. With a gurgle it sank to its knees and toppled over in the shallow water. Tenko and Birno bounded towards it. Birno dragged the warm carcass out of the stream. They each lifted it by two of its feet and struggled to the bank above them. It was a hard haul to carry it to the Bay of Skaill and by the time they got there the sun was lowering to the west.

"Meat! We have brought you meat!" Tenko cried.

The others greeted them with joy. They were hungry and shivering in the bitter wind.

"Let us skin the deer and eat it at once," Birno said.

"Listen, Birno," Lemba said. "While you and Tenko were away I went with Brockan to the huts at Skara. The sandbanks are round and over them but there is a hole at the top of your hut, though it is nearly full of sand inside. Still, I managed to get down into the hut and there is a little space beneath the overlapping walls where we might shelter for the night. There, perhaps, we might light a fire. Kali and Stempsi have gathered dry heather from the hills of Yettna." He pointed to a heap of kindling beside the boats. "We can fire the heather by rubbing two flints together." Lemba was expert at making sparks fly from two dry flints.

Birno frowned a little. "It is a slow, painful journey over the sand drifts and we have the deer to carry too."

Tenko laughed. "But there is an easier way! By the sea! Now we have the boats we can get there very soon." He pulled out his bronze axe. "Let us dismember the deer on this flat rock then the meat is more easily carried in the boat."

Quickly they cut up the deer and stowed the meat and the kindling in the boats. Birno and Stempsi took the smaller boat and Tenko, Lemba and the children the bigger one. Plying their paddles, they reached the shore below Skara.

It was a stiff climb up the shifting sand to the hut. It was like peering down a dark pit when they looked through the chimney hole. Birno lowered himself cautiously through it and fell with a soft thud on the soft sand below.

"It is not too far down and the fall is soft," he said. "I will catch you, Stempsi."

Stempsi climbed in and dropped into Birno's arms. Kali followed her, and then Tenko and Lemba dropped the deer meat and the kindling. Brockan went next, followed by Lemba and Tenko.

The sand sloped away in a pile to the sides of the hut, but all the beds and stone furniture were covered.

"At least we are out of the biting wind," Stempsi said. Though the storm had subsided, the breeze had shifted to the north and brought bitter cold with it.

Lemba, with the skill of the potter, struck his flints together and made sparks and kindled the dry heather. They had brought the bones of the deer and now impaled the meat on them and roasted it. They were desperately hungry and hardly waited for it to cook before they were tearing at it with their teeth. At last their hunger was satisfied and they began to talk.

"This is a shelter for the night but we can no longer live here," Birno said. "We could never manage to shift all this sand out of the hut."

Stempsi wept a little at the thought of all their treasures lost under the sand.

"It is plain we must go from here," Birno said.

"Where shall we go?" Lemba asked. "Shall we join some other tribe?"

Birno shook his head doubtfully. "They might not welcome us. Winter is drawing on and we have no food to take to them. It is sometimes hard enough to feed one's own people through a bad winter."

"Tenko could hunt for us," Brockan suggested.

"A deer every now and again would not be enough for us," Birno said. "There are not many deer on the hills of Orkney. We have the boats. Tenko has told us there are many forests full of animals in the land to the south. Could you take us to your own father's people, Tenko? Perhaps there we could learn to hunt?"

Tenko stared into the fire, thinking hard, then he shook his head.

"Listen, Birno ... all of you. I had to flee from my own country because of the war between my tribe and a neighbouring one. I saw my father killed. Our enemies pursued me to the shore but I managed to escape in our boat. One tribe was always fighting another to take their hunting grounds. The forest there did not seem big enough for all of us. The kindness of the gods brought me to your shores and here I found ways of peace. Your tribes live in friendly fashion, one with another. Lokar taught me new thoughts and ways. It is better to be herdsmen with sheep and cattle than hunters always on the prowl. No, there is no future for us in the land I left. I do not want to go back there. My tribe there is dead."

"Where then can we go?" Stempsi cried in despair.

"I have always wanted to find men who knew the secret of making bronze axes like this one," Tenko said slowly. "Maybe we could go in search of them?"

Birno was beginning, "But that is just a foolish dream, Tenko..." when he remembered Lokar's words. *Do not scorn Tenko because he is young. He will know what to do.* "Where then would you go, Tenko?" he asked instead.

"There is enough meat to last us three days if we do not eat greedily," Tenko remarked. "Tomorrow, if the sea is calm, let us load the meat into the boats and pull to the north. There are islands to the far north. I think the man of Saebar called them the Shetland Isles. To them people have come from across the great sea to the east. He said there were not many of them but they kept sheep and they knew how to make axes of bronze. Perhaps they will welcome us as they are only a small tribe. Will you go there with me, Birno, to find out?"

Birno drew a deep breath. "Yes, I will go, Tenko. The future is with you and Kali, yes, and with Brockan. We will adventure to the northern isles together. And now let us sleep under the shelter of these walls for the last time, for we have far to go in the days ahead."

The next day they pushed out the boats into the Bay of Skaill and watched the sand dunes that covered Skara grow smaller and dimmer as they headed northwards.

"Farewell, Skara, for ever!" Kali said sadly.

"Not for ever, Kali! Lokar said the same power that overwhelmed it would restore it, but it would not be in our time," Tenko told her. "For us there will be a new life. Take your paddle and pull with a brave heart."

Kali gave Tenko a look of trust and love. She took her paddle and matched her stroke to his as they pulled away to the north and to the new life they sought.

The Boy with the Bronze Axe is the ideal book for exploring the Stone Age and Skara Brae in classrooms.

You can find inspiring teacher resources and pupil worksheets themed for the book at **discoverkelpies.co.uk**

Also by Kathleen Fidler

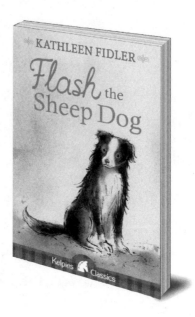

Flash the sheep dog is loyal, clever and brave. Before Flash arrived, orphan Tom was lonely and bored living on his uncle's sheep farm in the remote Scottish Borders.

Tom thinks his best friend could be a sheep dog champion so together they train for the sheep dog trials. But on the day of the big competition Tom faces a difficult decision – go to America, or stay with Flash?

A heart-warming story of friendship, acceptance and finding a place to call home.

 Also available as an eBook

discoverkelpies.co.uk

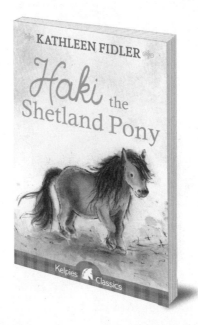

Crofting lad Adam teaches his best friend Haki to do things other Shetland ponies can't – act, dance and even follow the sound of Adam's bagpipes!

When Adam has to leave Shetland he knows he can't take Haki with him. At one last Highland Show, they meet a circus ringmaster looking for a special Shetland pony for a new act – will Adam and Haki begin a new life in the circus?

This classic children's tale is full of adventure, friendship and Scottish charm.

 Also available as an eBook

discoverkelpies.co.uk

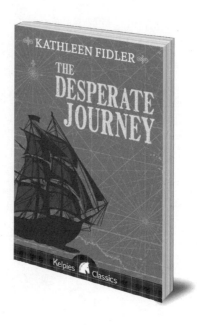

Twins Kirsty and David Murray are forced to leave their crofting home in the north of Scotland, and struggle to cope with life in Glasgow, where the work is hard and dangerous. Then comes a chance for a new adventure on a ship bound for Canada.

Will they survive the treacherous Atlantic crossing, and what will they find in the strange new land?

The Desperate Journey, a true Scottish classic about the Highland Clearances, is Kathleen Fidler's best-known story.

 Also available as an eBook

discoverkelpies.co.uk

You may also enjoy

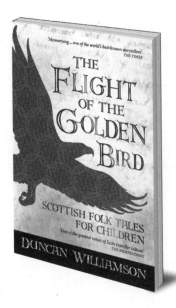 

Meet hunchbacked ogres and beautiful unicorns, brave princesses and magic scarecrows in two enchanting collections of tales from great Scottish storyteller Duncan Williamson.

You'll love these wonderful folk and fairy tales, collected from sixty years of travelling around Scotland.

 Also available as eBooks

discoverkelpies.co.uk

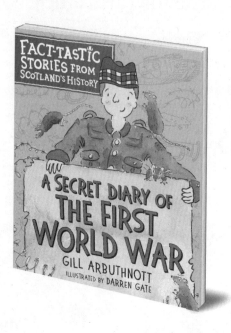

Step into the boots of 14-year-old soldier James Marchbank to find out what the First World War was really like.

Why was rat hunting a popular hobby in the trenches?
How did parachuting pigeons help win the war?
Why would a really good friend rub whale oil on your feet?
What did it really feel like to be a teenager at war?

Take a journey through time and discover all the most important and incredible bits of the First World War.

Inspired by the real-life diary of a Scottish boy soldier.

 Also available as an eBook

discoverkelpies.co.uk

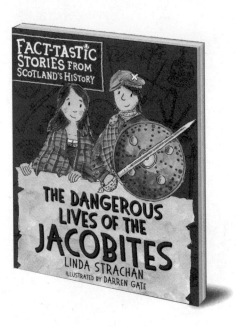

Step into the shoes of brother and sister, Rob and Aggie, to find out what it was really like to live in the Scottish Highlands and fight for the Jacobites.

Who was Bonnie Prince Charlie?
Why were bagpipes classed as a Weapon of War?
What really happened at the Battle of Culloden?
How did the Jacobite Risings change Scotland forever?

Includes maps, timelines, family trees and more!

 Also available as an eBook

discoverkelpies.co.uk

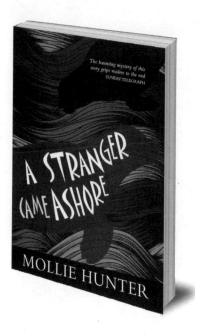

When Finn Learson staggers out of a stormy sea into a village on the Shetland Isles, he brings a secret with him. While the other villagers are enchanted by the stranger, Robbie suspects he's hiding something.

Haunted by tales of the Selkie Folk, Robbie sees clues everywhere – the strange coin, the missing ship, Finn's love for Robbie's sister and her golden hair. But can Robbie convince the others in time to save his sister?

 Also available as an eBook

discoverkelpies.co.uk

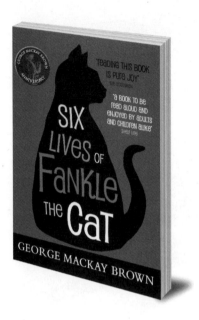

'Reading this book is pure joy.' – *The Scotsman*

When the shopkeeper gives Jenny a skinny, black kitten
she has no idea that Fankle is no ordinary cat. The fiercely
clever feline tells her of the six lives he has lived so far: lives
of adventure, danger, fortune and poverty.

So what is he doing living in a crofter's cottage in Orkney?

This classic novel by George Mackay Brown is a rich and
rewarding read for adults and children alike.

 Also available as an eBook

discoverkelpies.co.uk

'Glorious for sharing... Guaranteed wonder-full.' – *The Guardian*

Hamish and Mirren live in a quiet farmhouse by a beautiful loch in Scotland. Quiet, that is, except for the talking sea urchin, singing sand, hungry fairies, sad bogle and grumpy witch!

This delightful collection of stories is a true Scottish children's classic. Moira Miller's stories are full of wit and humour while *Katie Morag* creator Mairi Hedderwick's funny, charming illustrations bring gentle Hamish and his canny wife wonderfully to life for young readers.

 Also available as an eBook

discoverkelpies.co.uk

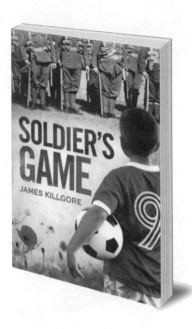

'Brings to life a small slice of Great War history.'
– *The Scotsman*

Young football fan Ross is amazed when he discovers that his great-grandfather Jack played for his favourite team, the famous Heart of Midlothian FC.

As Ross finds out more about Jack, an incredible story unfolds – a tale of Edinburgh's young heroes and a battalion of footballers and fans who fought in the First World War.

Based on the remarkable true story of the 16th Royal Scots, known as the "Hearts Battalion".

 Also available as an eBook

discoverkelpies.co.uk

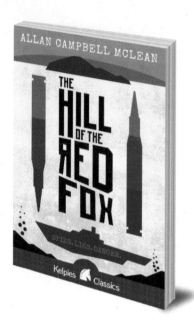

It's the Cold War. Soviet spies are feared, and secrets are traded. People disappear.

Thirteen-year-old Alasdair, from London, knows nothing about spies and secrets. On his way to claim a croft on the Isle of Skye left to him in his father's will, a stranger slips him a mysterious note before leaping from a moving train.

Gradually adjusting to the tough life on Skye, Alasdair is not prepared for the web of danger and espionage that unfolds around him. Can he trust anyone on the island?

 Also available as an eBook

discoverkelpies.co.uk